The Curious Vanishing of Beatrice Willoughby

By G. Z. Schmidt

Printed and bound in April 2024 at Sheridan, Chelsea, MI, USA
www.holidayhouse.com
First Edition
3 5 7 9 10 8 6 4 2

Cataloging in Publication Data is available from the Library of Congress.

ISBN: 978-0-8234-5073-2 (hardcover)

For my husband, forevermore

Chapter One

Few people visited the Amadeus residence after the Incident. The mansion was situated deep inside the Inkwoods, an ancient forest of black trees that blocked sunlight year-round. Each tree had gnarled branches that twisted in every direction and brittle leaves the color of black ash. There were no chirping birds or furry squirrels or any of the other friendly things that accompanied regular forests. Instead, the Inkwoods were dead silent, day and night. The only hints of life were the faint spiderwebs dangling from the branches and blanketing the rotting tree stumps.

The Amadeuses were a middle-aged couple. Mort Amadeus had black hair, a matching black cloak, and a slight frown, as if anything a person said or did would annoy him. His wife, Maribelle, had curly hair that was golden like the sun and a secretive smile, as if anything a person said or did would amuse her. Both adults were ghoulishly pale, their eyes a dreary gray. They lived with Mort's elderly mother, Edie, a seamstress who only communicated by sewing words through her embroidery.

The Amadeuses had always been considered somewhat strange. Before the Incident, the family had been strange but also popular. Every October, they held an impressive All Hallows' Eve party at their mansion. Their parties were a longtime favorite among the townspeople nearby, with a bit of something for every kind of person. For music lovers, there were impressive melodies playing from instruments that had been enchanted to perform by themselves. There were tall platters of food that satisfied even the pickiest eaters. And there were all sorts of conversations happening in every corner, with topics ranging from the intricate philosophy of trick-or-treating to the weather.

And, most memorable of all, there were lovely marionettes dangling from the walls and ceilings, each eerie, grinning toy dressed in a special costume. Maribelle was said to be the genius behind the creation of these puppets, with Mort as her helpful assistant who glued on the strings and wooden handles, and Edie the one who helped sew the little top hats and petticoats and trousers. Some guests claimed the puppets bore a strange resemblance to people they knew, but they could never be sure. At the end of each party, every guest was allowed to buy a puppet and take it home as a souvenir.

The grown-ups in town looked forward to the event each year. Gentlemen purchased expensive suits months in advance, and ladies bought glittering jewels in the shape of tiny skulls or spiders. Parents booked babysitters as early as June.

It all stopped after six-year-old Beatrice Willoughby vanished at one of the Amadeuses' parties.

For a while, the name Beatrice Willoughby brought about mournful murmurs and whispers throughout the town. *Poor thing. Tragic case.* Later, when Mort was connected with her disappearance and arrested, the townspeople were divided on what to think. *Mort is innocent, he's a kind man,* some insisted. Others claimed there was always something off about the family. *Odd folks, full of dark magic. Their house* is *the last place Beatrice was seen, after all. . . .*

The whole thing happened thirteen years ago. After the arrest, the Amadeuses became exceedingly private. They closed their doors and cast an enchantment over their residence so that no one could find their house. Several times a year, a handful of explorers would venture bravely into the Inkwoods (usually after imbibing one too many ales at the local tavern). They'd emerge from the dark trees hours later, babbling incoherently about endless mazes and talking bats.

Nobody had seen or heard from the family for ages. Then, thirteen years later, on the Monday morning before All Hallows' Eve, six households in town received an invitation to a special gathering at the Amadeus mansion.

Dear friend,

We cordially invite you to a celebration this Saturday evening, the 31st of October, at the Amadeus household. We've provided clear instructions below on how to find our address. (Otherwise, we're afraid you'll get dreadfully lost like those poor travelers last month.)

The party starts at eight o'clock sharp. Please RSVP by placing this letter back in your mailbox by Friday at midnight.

Yours,

The Amadeuses

The curious thing about people is how their curiosity eclipses everything else. All the invitees eventually accepted. They were old friends and enemies and strangers. One was an heiress, one was a spy, and one was an alchemist.

Innocuous, sure.

There was also a thief and an impostor. Another invitee had the ability to hypnotize people. One could see the future. And one could resurrect dead birds.

Oh, and lastly, at least one of the invitees was the true culprit responsible for the disappearance of Beatrice Willoughby thirteen years ago.

Chapter Two

SATURDAY, OCTOBER 31
EIGHT HOURS UNTIL MIDNIGHT

On Saturday afternoon, on a street near the town entrance, the plump, elderly innkeeper of the gray-and-black Victorian house labeled NEVERMORE INN slipped outside to inspect her porch, which she did fifteen times a day. She muttered to herself.

"Oh crows, oh no."

Mrs. Raven used her handkerchief to dab away a piece of pink bubblegum from the front porch. Those unkempt kids from room 201 must have done it; they'd been smacking the dreadful candy since they'd arrived with their family a few days ago, rubbing their sticky fingers everywhere: the staircase, the furniture, the stuffed crows in the entryway. She thought parents would be keeping a closer eye on their children, especially after what had happened to that Dutch boy the other day, but no.

The Nevermore Inn was packed, as usual. The small town of Nevermore was located in a remote part of Europe, hidden between tall, wide mountains, but that didn't stop tourists from finding it. Every day, awestruck visitors crowded the cobblestone streets as they took photos of the charming cottages and asked locals about the Inkwoods. The town was especially crowded during the last week of October, when the trees along the sidewalks were bright orange, and the air smelled of apples and cinnamon.

And of course, there was All Hallows' Eve.

It was Mrs. Raven's least favorite day of the year: All Hallows' Eve, the holiday when greedy children would dress up as ghoulish monsters and ring her doorbell for candy and leave muddy footprints all over her front porch. She shuddered at the thought, especially the thought of candy—sticky bubblegum and sugary lollipops and melting chocolates. She had a toothache just picturing it. If only the tradition involved giving children spinach casseroles or turnip pies.

"Today, things will be different," she muttered. Yes, she could feel it in her old bones.

Twenty minutes later, she had finally scrubbed the front porch spotless. She tucked her chin under her autumn shawl and grabbed her bags with her special tools.

As she headed down the street, she heard a voice call, "Mrs. Raven? Mrs. Raven, is that you?"

A lady in an enormous plum-colored dress and matching gloves was making her way outside a neighboring brown-and-white cottage. Her posture was stick straight, and her voice had a measured air to it, as though she were much better than you and knew it perfectly well. A velvet hat swelling with purple flowers was perched on her head, its black veil hiding her porcelain-white face. None of the townspeople, including Mrs. Raven, had ever seen the duchess without her veil.

Mrs. Raven stopped walking and gave a polite smile. "Good afternoon, Duchess von Pelt."

"It *is* a good afternoon," replied the duchess, crossing the street to join the elderly woman. "This town has wonderful autumns."

"Yes, I—"

"Now, the autumns in France are something else. This was in the south on my family's château, during my teenage years. . . ."

The duchess went on to recount her youthful memories while Mrs. Raven nodded and said, "Uh-huh," every so often. It was a trick the innkeeper had learned from serving guests for fifty years. An innocent smile, a nod of the head, and an agreeable murmur ("You don't say!") was enough to fool the other person into thinking you were paying close attention while your mind was free to wander.

Ten minutes later, the duchess finally paused to catch her breath. "Are you doing anything amusing for All Hallows' Eve?"

Mrs. Raven snapped out of her daydream about dead birds and cheese. "Actually, tonight—"

"I suppose you'll be busy tending to all the tourists," finished Duchess von Pelt with a sympathetic nod. "I, on the other hand, will be spending the evening at—hear this—the *Amadeus* household."

"You're going to see the Amadeuses?" Mrs. Raven asked with a hint of surprise.

"Yes, they've invited me!" said the duchess with a bright smile. Because of the duchess's veil, Mrs. Raven could only see her bright-red lips and white teeth. "I haven't been to their house since the Incident. I received the most thoughtfully delivered invitation on Monday. It arrived alongside a beautiful bouquet of roses, almost as beautiful as myself....I imagine the Amadeuses found me charming—most people do—and longed to see me after all this time. At any rate, their All Hallows' Eve parties never used to be invitation-only; I'm glad they're taking a step in the right direction. A *proper* party always has a specific guest list. Otherwise any *riff-raff* can attend...."

Finally, to Mrs. Raven's great relief, the duchess glanced at her watch and exclaimed she was late for an appointment at the cobbler's. "I must be off; it's nearly five o'clock. Talk another time!"

Mrs. Raven muttered goodbye. "Oh crows, I've been talking for twenty minutes," she grumbled to herself. "Or rather, *she's* been talking for twenty minutes while I listened! Hmph."

The old innkeeper headed to the marketplace in a foul mood. The town center bustled with locals and tourists. Merchants sat with their carts bursting with goods: peaches in every shade of the rainbow; paintings of the surrounding mountains that changed from sunrise to sunset, depending on the time of day; lacy doilies spun from the silk of the Inkwoods' spiders. Gossiping customers trickled in and out of the tavern. Mrs. Raven pulled out a shopping list from her pocket.

Milk
Butter
Sugar
Salt
Thick wire (hard to bend)
Thin wire (easy to bend)
New black thread
Fresh dead bird

As she shopped, however, her mind was somewhere else. She had not mentioned to the duchess that she, too, had been invited to the Amadeus household that night.

Like the duchess, Mrs. Raven had been surprised to

find her invitation in the mail earlier that week. Hers did not arrive with a rose bouquet (Mrs. Raven had no patience for the thorny flowers), but instead, a sleek black feather had been enclosed in the envelope. The last time the innkeeper had gone to the Amadeuses' place had also been thirteen years ago. Mrs. Raven's memory was as sharp as a crow's, and she vividly remembered the night of the party.

The party had started out as it did every year. Guests filled the grand mansion, dressed in their finest outfits. Nobody wore silly costumes or ate candy. The event was a strictly formal affair—the way All Hallows' Eve *should* be. As usual, Mrs. Raven had brought along one of her famous pies, which she brought to every party. She remembered mingling with the many guests. She recalled bumping into the loud and boisterous Mayor Willoughby, who was bragging about the brand-new swimming pool he had installed in his backyard over the summer.

Mrs. Raven remembered the duchess later arguing with the mayor over salad forks. She remembered an enthusiastic traveler who had the perfect (though sometimes long-winded) tale for every situation he encountered at the party. The hosts and guests had smiled politely as they waited for him to finish.

Usually there were no kids present, but that year Mayor Willoughby had brought along his six-year-old daughter, Beatrice. Mrs. Raven remembered when the others first realized Beatrice Willoughby had gone missing. Investigators had swarmed the house late that evening. Like every other guest, Mrs. Raven had been peppered with questions, and she barely managed to leave the place amid the chaos.

Now, thirteen years later, she pondered on the peculiar invitation. "But I thought Mort was still in prison," she said to herself as she examined a cart of overripe apples. "He must have been released. . . . That must be why they're hosting the parties again. . . ." Strange. She hadn't heard word of his release. Mrs. Raven had her special way of knowing such things that went on in the town, such as the fact that the duchess wore gloves because she had sticky fingers—and not because of bubblegum—or that Judge Ophelius used to accept bribes of rare books in exchange for doling out lenient punishments.

As Mrs. Raven turned the corner to one of the side

streets, she saw Dr. Foozle, the pharmacist, talking with a customer outside his shop. Their hushed conversation made Mrs. Raven halt.

"...and it kills without leaving residue?" the customer was saying. He was bent over in a long gray jacket that trailed past his feet, his top hat hanging low on his head, and his scarf wound so high around his neck that none of his skin was exposed to the chilly air.

"It is one of the only substances in the world that is virtually untraceable," said Dr. Foozle.

With a jolt, Mrs. Raven recognized the customer's voice. It was none other than the Amadeuses' mysterious caretaker, Wormwood. He had appeared in town shortly after the Beatrice Willoughby incident, running errands for the family. He had popped up in random places around Nevermore over the last twelve years, always dressed in that ridiculous ensemble. Mrs. Raven leaned in closer.

"It's colorless and odorless," Dr. Foozle continued. "Highly toxic. One swallow will kill a grown man. It has a few hours left to finish brewing."

"Superb," said the caretaker. "Bring it to the party tonight. I shall make good use of it."

The pharmacist said something inaudible. The caretaker laughed, but there was no humor in the laugh.

Oh crows, oh no. Mrs. Raven had an ill feeling she shouldn't be eavesdropping on this conversation. She tiptoed away quickly before either one saw her.

Outside the pharmacy, Wormwood and Dr. Foozle paused their conversation.

"I heard someone," said Wormwood, looking up the narrow street. He was a lanky fellow who moved with a jerking gait, as if his limbs were disjointed. His top hat tilted as his head turned, and his arms swung, almost hitting the pharmacist in the face.

Dr. Foozle dodged the caretaker and also glanced up the street. It was empty.

"We weren't talking about anything *too* incriminating," he reassured Wormwood nervously. But he decided it was best to change the subject. "Did you hear the latest gossip? An eight-year-old boy traveling with his family on vacation vanished at the Nevermore Inn."

"Yes, the family from Amsterdam," Wormwood replied. "He was last seen on the front porch, I hear. The parents have been searching the neighborhood."

"They won't have much luck there," remarked Dr. Foozle under his breath.

For as long as the townspeople could remember, various children between the ages of six and twelve had been disappearing around the town of Nevermore, one a year, always around All Hallows' Eve. They were usually kids of tourists and outsiders. The consensus was that they were unruly children who had run away from their parents. Certainly, the timing of these occurrences was a little unusual, but odd events were common in a town like Nevermore.

"If you ask *me*," added Dr. Foozle, "I think an inn is the best place for children to go missing."

"How so?"

"An innkeeper has access to all the rooms. Lots of opportunities to lock away troublesome kids."

"Are you talking about that old lady who runs the Nevermore Inn?" scoffed Wormwood. "Nonsense. The only thing she seems interested in are black birds."

Dr. Foozle adjusted his spectacles. "Well, it's no coincidence that many of the missing children's families were staying at her inn when they vanished."

"Only because it's the most popular place to stay for

tourists, Doctor." Wormwood paused, then asked, "Are the authorities going to investigate the missing kid?"

"Ah, probably not," said Dr. Foozle with a shrug. "A lot of tourists get lost when they travel. If they want to stay safe, then they shouldn't be traveling."

"That's like saying a lot of people choke when they eat, and that if they want to stay safe, then they should avoid eating." Wormwood's head rolled around from side to side. Dr. Foozle couldn't tell if it was a nod or a shake, but he suspected it was the latter.

Wormwood straightened himself. "It's interesting how there was a full investigation when Beatrice Willoughby disappeared," he remarked. "Yet there's been nothing done for these *other* missing kids. It's downright unfair, don't you think?"

"Ah, well, that's because Beatrice was the mayor's daughter," answered Dr. Foozle uncomfortably.

Mayor Willoughby was one of those people who wielded a lot of power and wasn't afraid to use it. If he passed a law forbidding lawns from growing past a certain height, he'd whip out his own ruler and measure every blade of grass just to find the one that was a centimeter too long, then force the owner to pay a hefty fine.

It was part of the reason the mayor had stayed in power for a much longer term than was normal. None of the townspeople had dared to challenge him.

Still, the Beatrice Willoughby incident was certainly tragic. That was what Dr. Foozle reminded himself at the end of every month, when he was forced to pay enormous taxes to the mayor.

Wormwood made a *tsk* sound behind his gray scarf. "I'll never understand humans."

Dr. Foozle sighed. "I had the perfect solution to prevent lost kids. . . . If only the stupid bureaucrats at the health board hadn't gotten involved."

For a while, Dr. Foozle had sold special bottles of liquid that turned the drinker neon pink as a way for parents to easily keep an eye on their children at all times. Unfortunately, there had been some trouble reversing the effects, and the local health board banned the substance. To this day there are several people living around the world with glowing pink skin.

"I have to go," the caretaker said. "There are a few things I must take care of. Remember, bring the vial tonight."

"Ah, will do."

Wormwood turned and headed down the path, his jacket trailing behind his rigid footsteps on the cobblestones. Dr. Foozle watched him disappear, then returned inside his pharmacy.

On the outside, the pharmacy looked like a humble, quiet little shop. But if you looked closely, you'd notice purple smoke wafting out of the chimney, and you'd notice the signpost above the door had a painted cauldron with green bubbles floating out of it. A nameplate above the mail slot read, in shiny letters, DOCTOR V. FRANKENSTEIN IV FOOZLE. (It was much easier, you see, that he simply went by Dr. Foozle.)

If you went past the entrance, you'd quickly realize it was no usual pharmacy. There were no white plastic bottles of pills or boxes of cough syrup. Instead, there was an enormous display of brilliantly colored bottles and vials. There were bottles of sunlight so that people could grow their flowers at night. There were sleeping drafts made of starlight and glass vials of lightning. Some of the bottles contained sparkling concoctions that changed colors every minute.

Dr. Foozle went to the back room of the shop, where he kept his most valuable stuff. Nested on the tables were jars of herbs, powders, bones, eyeballs, smiling lips, and other ingredients. He picked up a cylindrical glass tube of fine white powder. If the holder viewed it under the light at exactly the right angle, the dust appeared to glisten like diamonds.

Bone dust was an extremely rare substance. The name might suggest one simply needs to grind up some animal bones—perhaps the leftover chicken bone from the soup you had for lunch—but as every alchemist knows, it's not that simple. Not only did Dr. Foozle have to find oddly specific bones (among them the skull of a snake and the hind leg of a crocodile), but he also had to let them sit in the moonlight for twenty-one nights in a special brew that contained the sneeze droplets of a unicorn.

"Almost ready," the pharmacist murmured anxiously as he examined the glittering tube. In his flustered state, he accidentally knocked over a bottle of thunderstorm. A deafening crash echoed in the shop before he quickly plugged the cork back in.

Bone dust was also highly illegal. It had several magical properties, the most well-known being that it was a good way to kill someone stealthily—such as dissolving a spoonful in their cup of evening tea. The bureaucrats at the local health board would close his pharmacy for good if they knew he was brewing bone dust. But the caretaker had paid him handsomely, and it was worth the risk.

It was even worth the risk of going back to the Amadeuses' residence, especially after the Incident. On the corner of Dr. Foozle's desk was a tall glass bottle, the inside swirling with bright, flaky confetti. The invitation from the Amadeuses had arrived in the bottle, along with a fat envelope of cash for the bone dust.

"Yes, it's certainly worth the risk," Dr. Foozle reminded himself. *Why* the caretaker needed bone dust, the pharmacist had no idea. Normally, he asked his customers what their plans were before he sold them a potion or concoction. But he had not asked Wormwood.

Sometimes it was better to be kept in the dark about such matters.

Chapter Three

SEVEN HOURS UNTIL MIDNIGHT

On the other side of town sat a small yellow-and-white cottage. The shutters underneath its sloping rooftops were tightly closed. It was the only house on the street with no flower boxes or manicured lawn. Instead, the grass had been entirely replaced by gray rocks.

Past the thrice-locked door, the only light in the house came from the glow of the computer screen behind a mountain of legal textbooks and case studies.

The dark wood floors were littered with scrolls, pens, and more books. The books were long, obscure texts, with titles such as *The Unabridged Encyclopedia of Nouns,* or *An In-Depth Analysis of the Color Gray,* or *Theoretical Economics.*

In the middle of the cluttered room was a cushioned chair, upon which sat an aged man. Wrinkles were etched deep in his skin. A powdered white wig sat on his head, the curls brushing his shoulders.

The doorbell rang.

"Confound it," Judge Ophelius muttered, looking up from the law he was drafting. He had sent the mailman a stern letter instructing him to never ring the doorbell.

And yet, the doorbell rang again. And again. That was strange. Once meant a message, twice meant a salesperson, three times meant a visitor.

Judge Ophelius grabbed his walking cane. Hardly anyone visited him. Slowly he made his way to the front door. He peeked through the peephole.

There was no one there.

Judge Ophelius slowly unlocked the door and opened it. He shrank back from the late afternoon sun.

When his eyes finally adjusted, he saw a folded note on his porch.

He picked up the note. It was a handwritten letter, inscribed in thick black ink:

In case you're having second thoughts about tonight,
Your Honor, don't.

Judge Ophelius stared at the piece of paper. He looked up again. The only people out in the quiet neighborhood were his neighbor, Lady MacGrady, who was watering the flowers on her windowsill and talking with the town florist. The two were discussing a recent string of tulip thefts.

"Judge Ophelius!" Lady MacGrady called upon seeing him. "Just the person we wanted to see. Someone's been stealing the tulips from my windowsill!"

"Someone stole the tulips from my stall an hour ago, too," chimed in the florist.

"I'm sorry to hear that happened," the judge replied.

"This has *been* happening for much too long!" the florist said. "First the thief went for the roses. Then they started stealing the geraniums, too."

"Don't forget the lilies a few years ago!" added Mrs. MacGrady. "You'll catch this crook, won't you, Judge Ophelius?"

People were always asking Judge Ophelius for favors. He was, after all, the only judge for miles around. He also happened to be one of the best judges in the country. There were countless books and documentaries featuring some of his cases, the most famous of which involved a huntsman who had been convicted of killing a wolf that he claimed had disguised itself as a human in order to lure someone's granddaughter to her doom. The only evidence in the trial had been a piece of a red cape belonging to the girl.

"I will notify the authorities about this incident when I have time," the judge said politely, even though he already knew the police station always threw those cases out, citing more important crimes that occupied their time.

Judge Ophelius glanced at the piece of paper again. "By the way, did either of you see someone at my doorstep just now?"

The two people shook their heads. "I might've seen something fly past," said Lady MacGrady. "A bird, I think."

"It was bigger than a bird," argued the florist. "It looked like a flying rat."

"Hmm, I see. Thank you." The judge folded the piece of paper and went back indoors.

He glanced at the clock on the wall. Three more hours until the party.

When Judge Ophelius had first received the invitation on Monday, he wasn't sure if he would attend. Even the inclusion of a rare, gold-bound textbook with the invitation had not swayed him right away. Of all the cases Judge Ophelius had presided over, the Beatrice Willoughby case was the one that made him wince whenever he thought of it. He had tried to push it to the very back of his mind, burying it beneath new cases and the mundane, busy goings-on of everyday life.

It wasn't the details of the case that made the judge grimace. He'd presided over thousands of cases in his lifetime, some of them so foul they made his wig crawl and his skin itch. The Beatrice Willoughby case, all things considered, had been quite straightforward: a simple disappearance.

Then why did he feel so guilty?

He smoothed out the note from earlier and read the ominous message again.

Now the past had caught up to him, no doubt about it. The only thing worse than showing up would be *not* showing up.

He stood in front of the mirror and adjusted his black judicial robes. "The truth always comes out in the end," he said. "I only hope they can forgive me for what I did. . . ."

It was time for the judge to be judged.

Chapter Four

SIX HOURS UNTIL MIDNIGHT

In the crowded town center, festivities were beginning for All Hallows' Eve. Candlelit pumpkins illuminated the streets, nestled next to lifeless scarecrows that stared at the passersby. Small children with painted faces crowded around the merchant stalls, pointing excitedly at the caramel apples and pumpkin tarts. Older children wore masks and swapped spooky stories to scare their companions. The sun slowly sank into the horizon, smearing the sky with orange and pink hues.

Among the crowd was a gaunt man in a peacoat. Occasionally, as he walked down the streets, he'd take out a glistening pocket watch. He quietly squeezed through the marketplace and stopped in front of two teenagers who were waiting in line to bob for apples.

The man took out his pocket watch again. *Nineteen seconds.*

"I advise you to leave this line and go do something else," he told the teenagers in a bored tone.

They gave him a startled look. "Why?" one of them asked.

Thirteen seconds. The stranger yawned. "I recommend you do so immediately," he said. "That is, if you don't want to waste an entire bottle of shampoo later."

"Leave us alone, loser," the second teen said disdainfully.

Six seconds. The man put away the pocket watch and turned away without a word.

After he left, the two teens snickered and rolled their eyes—*what a weirdo.* Suddenly, there was a loud whooping. An enthusiastic man dressed up as a garbage bag ran through the crowd. He flung pieces of trash everywhere he went: gum wrappers, banana peels, half-eaten leftovers.

The people around him jumped aside to dodge the projectiles. Before either teen could let out a gasp, a rotten, half-eaten tuna sandwich flew their way.

SPLAT.

The man in the peacoat didn't bother laughing, nor did he turn around and say, "I told you so." He simply continued walking down the street, looking incredibly bored. Now and then, he'd check his pocket watch, then tap on a passerby's shoulder and say things like, "Check under your bed tonight before you turn out the light," or "Avoid returning home on the main street," or "Watch your garden, or more of your tulips will get stolen." He didn't answer their confused questions, nor did he particularly care if they took his advice. In his experience, the fewer words he said, the better.

He passed the packed town tavern. Upon seeing the count approaching, the tavern owner, who was taking a break at the entrance, suddenly paled. "G-good evening, Count Baines," the tavern owner stammered to the brick wall, determined to avoid eye contact. "H-hope all is w-well today."

The townspeople didn't know much about Count Baines. But they knew one thing: the count seemed to bring bad luck wherever he went.

"I'd block the left exit if I were you," Count Baines replied without stopping. "A nonpaying customer is going to make a run for it in exactly"—the count took out his glistening pocket watch again—"thirty minutes and three seconds."

The tavern owner's smile wavered in relief. "Ah. That's it today, then?"

"Additionally, in three hours, the new waitress you hired is going to slip and break her arm while carrying a load of new plates up the stairs."

The owner dashed indoors like a frantic mouse escaping an angry cat.

Count Baines didn't *bring* bad luck, of course. He simply advised people about their impending bad luck. Not that most people could tell the difference. *Simpletons,* he thought.

The count passed the cobbler's shop. A long line of customers waited outside the door.

"How many more minutes?" one of them grumbled.

"Thirty-nine minutes and fifteen seconds," Count Baines replied. The customer blinked at him.

One of the people emerging from the shop was Duchess von Pelt. "Hello, Count Baines!" the duchess said with a giant smile as she waved him over. "I was just picking up my high heels for an important party later tonight. The cobbler does a good job mending shoes, although I don't know if the materials he uses are *quite* up to par. . . ."

As the duchess talked about an Italian shoemaker she'd once known, a pair of children hurried past, struggling to carry a large bucket of candy. Scenes flashed before Count Baines's eyes, like images from a silent movie.

The boy tripped, spilling his bucket all over the sidewalk. Half of the candy landed in a dark puddle. Distressed, they tried to put the soggy remains back inside their bucket. Four minutes.

A short man in a brown suit walked past. The count blinked, and the scene in his mind changed.

The man in the brown suit headed down a dark alley. Suddenly, a mugger wrestled him to the ground and grabbed his wallet, then knocked him out for good measure. Fifteen minutes.

"Hello?" said Duchess von Pelt, waving her gloved hand in front of the count's face. "Did you hear what I said, Count Baines?"

Count Baines returned to the scene before him. "I have to go," he said tonelessly. "Don't bother asking the cobbler to mend your shoes. They'll break down again in"—he checked his pocket watch—"two hours and thirty-five minutes."

"What? Well, that's a shame. I've already paid him. . . ." The duchess frowned. "Anyhow, I should get going, too. As I've mentioned before, I have a special event to attend tonight."

The count managed a stiff smile as the duchess disappeared into the crowd. He knew about the special event Duchess von Pelt spoke of—his own invitation was crumpled at the bottom of his coat pocket.

He continued down the path, trying not to think of one particular scene that kept replaying in his mind. *A broken teacup, a high-pitched scream. An All Hallows' Eve party gone wrong.*

He checked his pocket watch. *Four and a half hours.*

Chapter Five

FIVE HOURS UNTIL MIDNIGHT

Inside the cobbler's store, the customers crowded around the workbench. Around them were shelves and shelves of shoes, shoes of all sizes and types—leather boots, sleek running shoes, high heels with twirly laces.

One customer, a tourist with a rosy headscarf, asked the others how long the cobbler had been in business.

"This shop has been here since I was young," croaked an elderly customer.

"Are you sure? The cobbler doesn't look older than twenty!"

"I think he's at least fifty-three," someone else replied.

A voice piped up from behind the workbench, startling everyone. "Do you want me to replace the soles on these?" the cobbler said, looking up from the boots he was mending.

Mr. H was someone who faded into the background easily. He was a fairly nondescript person, one of those people whose face you don't quite remember after seeing it. All you'd recall is he had two eyes (brown, maybe, or hazel?), a nose, and a mouth. He was of medium height with a medium complexion. His clothes were as bland as oatmeal, and he spoke in a quiet, unassuming voice. People often forgot he was there, even if he was standing right in front of them.

Mr. H didn't mind. In fact, he hated attention. That was why he didn't care that nobody ever seemed to remember his full name.

After he closed the store for the night, the cobbler headed to the back room. The shelves there were also filled with shoes, but these weren't for wearing. These were bronzed—dipped in glossy paint and then mounted onto display panels, like sets of trophies. They gleamed beautifully around the room, the light reflecting off their metallic surfaces.

Mr. H sat down in a chair and tapped his unremarkable chin distractedly. He almost didn't notice the woman sitting in the corner, bent over a table stacked with papers.

"Ahem," she said, looking up from the homework she was grading.

Ms. H was the town's only schoolteacher. Like Mr. H, she was the sort of person who tended to fade into the background. Nobody knew how long she had been teaching—it could have been one year or fifty-five. Most days, her students simply forgot she was in the room, and as a result paid little attention to her, which explained the bright-red *F* circled at the top of most of their papers.

"Ready for the party tonight?" she asked.

Mr. H frowned. "I don't know, I'm still surprised that the Amadeuses are resuming their parties again after all these years," he said. "Considering what happened at their last one."

Mr. and Ms. H spent the next few moments

considering exactly that. Beatrice Willoughby's disappearance had caused a great disturbance in the town. Over the years, the townspeople had tried to speculate what had really happened the night she'd vanished. Beatrice had never been found. Some suggested she had been transformed at the party with a vile potion—turned into a toad, perhaps, or a pile of soot, and deposited outside. Others were certain that she was still somewhere in the Amadeus mansion, hidden behind a trapdoor underneath the floorboards.

"Mayor Willoughby was very convinced of Mort's involvement in the affair," said Mr. H. "He's still in prison, last I heard."

"Well, he *was* a likely culprit, since the disappearance occurred at his house. In fact, the whole family is suspicious. . . . I do wonder if they'll allow kids this year, after what happened. . . ."

The schoolteacher remembered teaching Beatrice Willoughby in class. She had been in school for less than a year before the Incident. The girl had been a difficult student—she actually paid attention and asked questions during the lessons instead of sitting numbly and staring out the window like the other kids. Curious children were a nuisance. Ms. H was happiest when the students in her school didn't learn anything at all. Knowledge, someone once said, was power—and the fewer children with power, the better. It was far less work that way.

Mr. H picked up a rag and absentmindedly began polishing a pair of bronzed boots. The finish was so shiny, it gave off a bright-red sheen. "The Amadeuses seem keen on having us there," he said.

Indeed, their invitation from the Amadeuses had arrived with a set of fine-tipped pens for Ms. H and a brand-new shoe stand for Mr. H—in other words, the perfect gifts for a schoolteacher and a cobbler.

Mr. H added, "I'd hate to refuse and appear rude. . . ."

"Me too," said Ms. H.

Mr. H looked up, his murky eyes concerned. "Is it safe, though? You don't think the Amadeuses are *up* to something tonight?"

Ms. H's equally murky eyes blinked as she considered the questions. "No. They probably want to sell more of their little puppets. The family must be strapped for cash after all these years. Nothing bad will happen. There will be too many people around."

Historically, the Amadeuses' parties drew large crowds. Both Mr. H and Ms. H enjoyed large crowds. A large crowd meant they could easily blend in and avoid conversations. Mr. and Ms. H both hated conversations, which was why both were keen on ending this one as soon as possible.

"I suppose it won't hurt to make an appearance, then," said Mr. H.

"No, it probably won't," agreed Ms. H. She went back to grading papers.

Chapter Six

FOUR AND A HALF HOURS UNTIL MIDNIGHT

A brown caravan tumbled down the road along the edge of the Inkwoods. The black trees blended with the inky sky above, their tops illuminated by the white moon, which hung in the night like a luminous rusting orb.

The driver parked the caravan on the side of the road, next to the trees. A freckly redheaded boy emerged from the vehicle, a pair of dirt-colored goggles on his head.

Dewey O'Connor was one of those kids other children avoided. Part of it was due to the weird goggles he always wore. Part of it was due to the fact he'd rather read a book instead of spend time playing games. Everywhere the eleven-year-old went, he carried a thick book under his arm.

He glanced warily at the trees. "Are you sure about this place, Dad?" he asked.

His dad, Chaucer, stepped out and looked at the woods with a hungry expression. "It's just how I remember it from thirteen years ago!" he said, scratching his red beard. He quickly went to examine the trees more closely. "Just look at the rotting branches. And these dead leaves!"

Dewey's dad was fascinated by magic and mysteries. The father-and-son duo traveled across the land in their caravan, stopping to explore small towns and villages that contained magic folklore. Dewey, on the other hand, found such oddities confusing. He preferred things to be orderly and systematic. Magic was too unpredictable.

"Isn't it unusual these trees are dead, yet still alive?" said Chaucer excitedly.

Dewey examined a fragile black leaf through his

goggles. "Yes. It seems anatomically impossible, but they look *undead.*"

They stepped into the woods. Immediately the moonlight was swallowed by the trees, and the night, already dark, turned pitch-black. Chaucer confidently flicked on his flashlight and led the way.

First, they moved this way, then that. They took eight steps forward, then five left, then three to the right. "I remember the house was somewhere here. . . ." Chaucer said as they circled the same tree twice. "But they must have changed it. . . . Hmm, maybe it's down here. . . ."

For the past few months, Chaucer had been telling Dewey nonstop about the last All Hallows' Eve party he'd attended at the Amadeus place. "It was the best party ever!" he'd said countless times, recalling stories of giant balloons and delightful snacks—from peanut-coated spiders, to fried lizard eggs, to tiny glasses of deep-red liquid that dripped suspiciously like blood ("It was only cranberry juice, I'm ninety-five percent certain," Chaucer had said). Unfortunately, he'd had to leave the party early thirteen years ago, and he was determined to stay the entire night this time.

Dead leaves crackled underneath their feet as they

treaded through the dark woods. Dewey started to get worried.

"Are you sure you know where it is, Dad?" he asked.

Suddenly, they collided into a dark, round figure.

"Oh crows!" An old woman in a shawl appeared before them. "I'm sorry, it's hard to see out here."

"No worries at all," said Chaucer. He reached out his hand. "Chaucer O'Connor. Pleased to meet you. This is my son, Dewey."

The old woman introduced herself as Mrs. Raven. She carried a steaming pie under one arm.

"You seem familiar," said Chaucer. He snapped his fingers. "I remember now! We met thirteen years ago at the Amadeuses' All Hallows' Eve party."

"Is that where you're headed tonight?" Mrs. Raven asked.

"Yes! Traveled miles and miles for it. I'm afraid I don't have a map of the Inkwoods. . . ."

"Nobody does," said the old woman. "The world's best cartographers have tried to map the Inkwoods to no avail. I believe the instructions on the invitation said it's the tenth hollow tree to the left from here, so let's see now. . . ."

"Invitation?" Dewey spoke up. "Is the party invitation-only?"

Neither adult paid attention to Dewey's question. Chaucer was jabbing away about the last time he'd been there.

"How was last year's party?" he asked Mrs. Raven as they approached a hollow tree.

"Last year's?" said Mrs. Raven. "There was no party last year."

"Really? That's odd, I recall people saying the Amadeuses host one every October." Chaucer scratched his beard. "They must've fallen ill. Perhaps they had the grippe."

Mrs. Raven gave him a skeptical look. "Do you not know?"

"Know what?"

"Oh crows. I don't know if you ought to bring your son along tonight. A little boy like him might go missing."

Behind them, Dewey fumed. *Little boy?* He wanted to tell her about the latest books he'd read, which included a textbook on aerodynamics and a thick novel by Dostoevsky. But there was a more pressing concern. "What do you mean 'go missing'?" he asked.

Mrs. Raven started to speak, but the three of them halted in front of a creaky pair of wrought-iron gates. Up ahead, the mansion came into view, its silhouette as dark and foreboding as the rest of the woods. Dewey was awed by the mansion's sheer size—it spanned the size of at least four regular houses. He had lived in his dad's caravan since the day he was born, and he couldn't imagine living in such a giant space.

Only two square windows were lit throughout the enormous building, giving it an abandoned feel. "Huh . . . this is not how I remember it," Chaucer said. "Used to be much more . . . what's the word? *Lively*."

They headed up to the front porch. Scraggly shrubs grew along the entrance, and impressive columns buried in ivy adorned the doors. Mrs. Raven carefully pressed the skull-shaped doorbell. A deep, hollow chime echoed across the grounds.

Dewey glanced nervously at his dad, who wore an eager grin on his face. "I feel apprehensive about this whole thing," Dewey said.

"You know I don't understand big words like that, son," said Chaucer.

A tall, lanky individual in a top hat and scarf answered the door.

"Good evening, Wormwood," said Mrs. Raven with a nervous smile.

"How'd you know my name?" asked the caretaker skeptically. "Have we met?" He seemed to talk with a frown, but the guests couldn't tell because his scarf and top hat obscured his face.

Mrs. Raven blushed and mumbled something incoherent. "We're here for the party," she said, changing the subject.

"You're dreadfully early."

"Are we?" Mrs. Raven checked her watch. "Only by twenty minutes . . ."

Wormwood held out his arm stiffly, his sleeve dangling over his hand. "Show me your invitations, please."

Mrs. Raven pulled out hers. The caretaker took the paper with his sleeve and examined it before giving a stiff nod. Then he turned to Chaucer and Dewey.

"Hello there, I don't remember you from last time," Chaucer said with a friendly wave. "I didn't get an invite.

I was under the impression these parties were open to everyone, like before."

"Why would you assume that?" Wormwood replied.

"Well, you know what they say about parties: the more the merrier!"

The caretaker folded his arms, the sleeves bending in odd places. "That's not always true. Besides, the guest list was carefully curated for tonight's event."

"Please check with the hosts," Chaucer insisted. "I'm sure they'd be happy to have me! I was at their party thirteen years ago."

"Let them in," agreed Mrs. Raven. *Better to travel in a group, like a flock of birds,* the innkeeper thought privately. There was a better chance of getting away if misfortune came—and misfortune always arrived on All Hallows' Eve.

Wormwood sighed impatiently. "I will *ask,* but only because I'm benevolent," he said. He stepped aside and let Chaucer and Dewey into the house.

Warm orange candlelight lit up the inside of the mansion. Its dim glow cast long, grotesque shadows over the furniture and floorboards. The guests followed the caretaker through the wide foyer and down the hallway.

Large tapestries and paintings decorated the walls, images of moonlit cemeteries and bare trees.

They turned a corner and Dewey gasped. Dangling in front of him was a puppet of a ballerina. It had a frozen grin on its face and large, unblinking eyes, its arms hanging limply at its sides.

"Oops," said Wormwood, and he quickly yanked the puppet away, breaking its strings. "Forgot to clean this up earlier."

Such was the length of the mansion that they didn't reach their destination until a full minute later. Wormwood slowly pushed open the door to what looked like a dining hall. A long, empty table sat in the middle of the room, surrounded by tall chairs. A warm fire crackled in the fireplace next to the table.

"I'm afraid the hosts are busy preparing for the party," said the caretaker. "Please make yourselves comfortable. I shall ask if the . . . *unexpected* . . . visitors may stay."

His tone made Dewey shrink. He looked at his dad, who seemed cheerfully oblivious to the fact they weren't welcome.

The doorbell rang again. The caretaker frowned and

remarked, "These wretched guests can't seem to follow instructions to arrive on time."

With that, he headed out of the room.

Duchess von Pelt prided herself on many things. For one thing, she always color-coordinated her outfits: gloves, dress, hat, and the occasional parasol. For another, she always arrived fashionably early to every party. It made the other guests think she'd been invited to come ahead of the scheduled time, which made them think she was special friends with the hosts, which in turn made her extra special. And being extra special was paramount.

The duchess walked down the path to the mansion, a glittering lantern in her hand. The lantern was adorned with yellow and pink flowers, matching the ones sewn on her enormous lavender dress. She looked up at the Amadeus residence. She supposed it was a charming house—not nearly as grand as the dozens of properties she owned, obviously, but impressive all the same. Duchess von Pelt adjusted her floral hat, then knocked on the door.

"Good evening," she said brightly when the caretaker opened the door. The duchess held up a gloved hand and gave a big smile underneath her veil. "I'm here for the party."

"You realize the invitation says the event starts at *eight* o'clock?" Wormwood said.

"Oh, darling, it's close enough," Duchess von Pelt replied.

"Close enough only counts in hand grenades. I cannot let in any more guests until the proper time."

"I trust you'll be gracious and let me in," said the duchess.

"You'll have to wait out here," the caretaker replied irritably. He started to close the door.

The duchess's bright smile did not flicker. She reached out and pressed against the door before it shut all the way. "Perhaps I wasn't clear before." Duchess von Pelt raised her veil, revealing the rest of her face, and repeated sweetly, *"I'm here for the party."*

The caretaker's face went blank behind his scarf. His body seemed to tense up. He opened the door wider and said, much more warmly than before, "Good evening, Duchess. Follow me, please."

Duchess von Pelt followed him down the hallway. She was not disturbed by the eerie decor (though she did find it rather distasteful). The duchess rarely worried or got scared. Things often went her way.

It had been a while since she had seen the Amadeuses in person. She hadn't been surprised when she received the invitation in the mail—she was, after all, quite popular and got invited to lots of parties. The real question was if the party would satisfy her. The duchess had high standards, after all.

"Please wait in the dining hall," the caretaker said, pointing down the corridor.

"I'll be right there," Duchess von Pelt sang. "I have to make a quick stop."

There was one place she always went first upon arrival to a party, and that was the restroom. After getting directions from the caretaker, the duchess entered the Amadeuses' large, circular bathroom on the first floor. Inside were several stone basins, the edges of which were lined with flickering candles and jars of roses, their petals ranging from dark red to inky black.

Duchess von Pelt stood over one of the sinks and blinked at her reflection in the candlelit mirror. Excellent; her veil was still carefully in place.

When Duchess von Pelt arrived at the dining hall,

her mouth dropped. She had not been the first to arrive. The innkeeper and a random redheaded man she'd never met were already in the room, chatting about birds. A boy in dirt-colored goggles sat by the table, reading a book.

"Hello, Duchess von Pelt," said Mrs. Raven. "I was just telling Chaucer here about the best way to mend a bird's wing."

"Very fascinating procedure," said the redheaded man, who was writing in a notebook. "You could have been a . . . what's the word? Someone who studies birds?"

"*Ornithologist,*" the boy said from the table without looking up.

The man put away his pen and notebook and extended a friendly hand to the duchess. "I'm Chaucer O'Connor."

"Pleased," Duchess von Pelt said, clutching Chaucer's hand as lightly as possible before removing hers quickly. She eyed the man's coat, which was filthy and full of patches. And to think she had spent hours carefully stitching flowers onto her best evening gown!

"You seem familiar," Chaucer said, studying the duchess's veiled face. "Have we spoken before?"

"I'm certain we haven't," said Duchess von Pelt, who couldn't imagine herself ever voluntarily speaking to a man like Chaucer.

Chaucer snapped his fingers a few times. "I remember now! You were here thirteen years ago, weren't you? You wore a huge dress that reminded me of a frosted cake. It looked kind of silly," he added with a laugh.

Duchess von Pelt exhaled sharply through her nose. Luckily, she was particularly skilled at appearing calm even in the most disastrous of situations, like the time another guest wore the same dress she had to a luncheon. The duchess gave a polite but icy smile.

"Chaucer's a traveling handyman," said Mrs. Raven. "He does all sorts of things: mends pots, rebinds books . . ."

"I'm also a story collector," Chaucer said. "I meet interesting people from my travels and write about them."

"Do you?" the duchess said, brightening up considerably.

"Yes, I have collected many stories over the years this way. My favorite is about the young man in Switzerland who walked around with neon-pink skin." Chaucer rubbed his beard, thinking. "Another intriguing story is the one about a family of witches who live in a swamp. Or... have either of you heard of the mysterious man who wins every game he plays?"

"What?" asked Mrs. Raven.

Chaucer nodded fervently. "In my travels, I've come across many reports of a stranger who walked into a chess tournament here, or a poker competition there. Games of skill, games of chance—he was a master of all of them. He'd come in first place, then vanish with his winnings before people could ask him any questions. One of the incidents happened not far from here, in fact. I have the story written somewhere." Chaucer took out his notebook and flipped through the pages until he found what he was looking for. He cleared his throat.

Once upon a time, there was a train where card players from all over gathered to play games as they rode along.

One group in particular was known as the Scarlet Hands. They were seasoned players, some of the best in the world, each with nimble fingers and a sharp mind. They also depended more on trickery than actual skills to ensure they'd win, and if deception came to fail, they resorted to other unsavory means, hence the name of their group. Unwitting passengers often challenged the Scarlet Hands, not realizing what they were getting themselves into. Some ended up losing their entire life savings in a single game.

Then one evening, a new passenger came aboard and decided to challenge the Scarlet Hands. Nobody knew where he had come from, only that the fellow looked extremely bored and often glanced at his watch.

One by one the players made their bets. Antes were raised. Cards were revealed. The newcomer won the first round, then the second, then the third. Nobody had seen anything like it. By the end of the night, the newcomer had won more money off the Scarlet Hands than anyone ever had before.

Now, the long-standing group members were having none of it. "Tell you what," one of the Scarlet Hands told the stranger, "next round will be double or nothing. You either double your winnings or lose everything you've won."

The stranger agreed with a yawn. The group members, meanwhile, slyly winked at each other. They weren't going to let this fellow take away all their money. They still had a few tricks up their sleeves.

They began a new round. The stranger took out his watch. Then, right before the last player put down his cards, the stranger said calmly, "That's including the ace of spades hidden in your left sleeve."

A stunned silence fell across the table. Nobody had ever been clever enough to call out the group's tricks. "Are you calling us cheaters?" they said threateningly.

The stranger merely yawned and glanced at his watch. "No, but I'm calling you a doctor," he replied.

Without warning, one of the players pulled out a knife and swung it at the stranger's head. But the stranger had already ducked. The knife hit the gas lantern on the wall. Flames engulfed the player's sleeve, and he howled in pain.

The awed onlookers asked the stranger who he was. But the stranger only yawned again, swept up his peacoat, and left the table. The train stopped at its next station, and the man was never seen again.

"What train was this?" asked Mrs. Raven, clutching her chest.

"It has been abandoned for years. It ran on a railroad track that now passes through empty towns." Chaucer closed his notebook. "It's funny how quickly things disappear."

Chapter Seven

FOUR HOURS AND TEN MINUTES UNTIL MIDNIGHT

A few feet away, Dewey wrinkled his forehead and tried to concentrate on his book as the adults in the room droned on.

"Oh crows, sounds like the man was psychic," Mrs. Raven was saying.

"Quite possibly," agreed Chaucer. "Imagine if you could see into the future. Chess games and card games would be a cinch!"

Their chatter proved distracting. Dewey put down his book and spoke up. "But Dad, seeing into the future is a paradox. If I were to tell you that tonight you will find a fifty-dollar bill, you'll go out of your way to look extra carefully in all the places you normally wouldn't. When you finally do find the money, it's only because you went and *searched* for it."

The grown-ups ignored him. "Fascinating story, Mr. O'Connor, but I've got even better ones," Duchess von Pelt said in a lofty voice. "If you want someone with interview experience, you'll be happy to know I've done *my* fair share for magazines and newspapers. . . ."

Deciding that nobody would miss his presence, Dewey went off in search of a quieter place to read. He knew his dad would be too busy being giddy about the party to notice he had disappeared.

The hallway outside the room was silent and empty. Dewey tried some of the doors to the other rooms, but they were all locked. As he reached the end of the long corridor, he came before a set of stairs. After he checked to make sure nobody was watching him, he went up the winding staircase.

It led to another landing, identical to the floor below.

Candles lit the dim hallway from the walls. Dewey briefly wondered how long it took the residents of the house to light all the candles each day. He slowed his pace, his footsteps creaking on the floorboards. He kept half expecting someone—or something—to jump out at him from the shadows.

The door to one of the rooms was ajar. Quiet voices came from within. Dewey stopped to listen.

"We went over the guest list carefully," a male voice said. Dewey recognized it as Wormwood's. "We must not deviate from it in any way."

"Don't be silly," a woman replied in a singsong voice. "Two extra guests won't ruin our plan. One of them is a little boy, you said?"

"Yes, but it's too dangerous, Maribelle," the caretaker argued. "Do you want another incident like Beatrice Willoughby's on our hands?"

"You're overreacting. Everything will be fine."

Their voices dropped to low murmurs. Dewey leaned in closer to hear. As he did so, the wood floor beneath his feet went *creak*.

The noise made the two grown-ups in the room abruptly stop talking.

"Did you hear that?" Wormwood asked.

Dewey froze. He couldn't get away now without making more noise.

"Just the house settling," said Maribelle. "You've been with us long enough to know it's a very old building." She gave a soft, tinkling laugh. "You're much too jumpy, Wormwood."

"Being cautious is a virtue—all humans could benefit from more caution. That is why I have misgivings about tonight."

"Stop worrying. Go keep an eye on the uninvited guests."

"If you insist, ma'am."

Dewey retreated just in time. He darted back down the corridor and ducked beneath a round table in the hallway. He realized that if he tucked his knees, he could hide on the bottom ledge of the table, out of sight. He held his breath as he watched Wormwood's long jacket glide past. Oddly enough, the caretaker's footsteps made no noise on the creaky floorboards.

Dewey waited until Wormwood was out of sight, his heart hammering as he pondered the conversation he had heard.

◂ ◂ ◂

Half a mile away, in the depths of the Inkwoods, Dr. Foozle opened his spare bottle of sunlight. Floating orbs of sunshine danced in the air above his head. Dr. Foozle walked onward cautiously, following the instructions to the mansion, which he'd memorized. He touched the tiny glass vial he'd placed inside his lab coat, nestled among the potions and brews he carried in case of emergencies. Good, it was still there.

There were no sounds except the soft thumping of his footsteps, the crinkling leaves, and the occasional crackling tree branch. It was, he realized, exactly the kind of place where people could disappear and never return.

Just follow the plan, he reminded himself. Get to the party, give Wormwood his purchase, then slip out early when nobody's looking.

Suddenly, his hair bristled on the back of his neck. He glanced up at the dark trees uneasily. There was nothing but layers of dead, rotting branches and leaves.

"Just the atmosphere," he mumbled to himself. He reached into his coat again and extracted a tiny bottle of bright blue liquid. The pharmacist uncorked the bottle and drank the contents in one gulp. His nervousness eased.

Dr. Foozle, like most of the townspeople, normally avoided the Inkwoods. Some kinds of magic were too great to disturb. He was always puzzled why anyone would choose to live in such a dark and secluded place. Maybe the Amadeuses were allergic to the sun. In that case, he could try selling them his latest allergy potion. It helped prevent allergies against almost everything, from bee stings to dragonfruits.

"Salutations, Doctor," said a voice behind him.

Bewildered, Dr. Foozle turned around to see a shadowy figure with a walking cane stumbling toward him.

"Judge Ophelius?" said Dr. Foozle, blinking in surprise. "Are you here for the party?"

"Affirmative," Judge Ophelius answered. He straightened the collar of his black judicial robes. "I don't get out much these days. Almost didn't come. But the hosts were insistent. . . ."

"The woods seem more ominous than usual, huh, Judge?"

"Well, Doctor, it *is* All Hallows' Eve."

It was common knowledge that All Hallows' Eve was the one time of the year when magic was at its strongest, when enchantments magnified tenfold. Silky strands of spiderwebs were extra sticky; the moonlight was extra bright. Age-old trees that hovered above the streets seemed extra ancient, reminding passersby of the decades of experience and wisdom their branches held. Spells that normally wouldn't work during other times of the year were cast easily on All Hallows' Eve.

Judge Ophelius peered curiously at the floating sun orbs, which were slowly fading into the dim, hazy colors of eventide. "Ah, yes. I remember approving those bottles of sunlight."

Judge Ophelius oversaw the local health board that Dr. Foozle hated. Over the years, the board had forbidden Dr. Foozle from selling countless potions that were deemed "unsafe for the public." It was one of the reasons Dr. Foozle was not too fond of the judge. A slight panic rose in his chest. *If he finds out about the illegal bone dust...*

"I haven't seen Mort or Maribelle in a long time," the pharmacist said lightly, trying to sound casual. "I suppose nobody has. It'll be good to see them again, won't it?"

The judge frowned. "Mort is still in prison."

"Ah. Is that so?"

They walked onward in silence.

"Doctor, why do you keep poking the inside of your jacket?" the judge asked curiously.

Dr. Foozle, who had been checking on his bone dust, quickly fumbled for a different vial. "Oh, I was just—I was wondering if you wanted some tonic water!"

"I beg your pardon?"

"I can sell some to you at a discount, if you'd like," babbled Dr. Foozle. "Great for curing stomachaches and nerves!" He produced a glinting orange bottle from his coat and uncorked it. "One drop will—wait, not this one—"

A bright, shimmering substance danced in the air before bursting in a flurry of tiny droplets resembling popping bubbles. By the time the stun powder subsided and the two men's eyes recovered from the flashes, blackened leaves and broken branches floated in midair, as if suspended by invisible strings.

Judge Ophelius rubbed his eyes. "What's the big idea?" he demanded.

"Ah, it was stun powder," Dr. Foozle coughed. "Sorry about that."

The trees nearby rustled. A gaunt, unsmiling man in a gray peacoat emerged onto the path.

"Count Baines?" said Dr. Foozle, surprised for the second time that night. "You're coming to the party, too?"

"Obviously," Count Baines said. His tone was neither friendly nor cold. He surveyed the rubble-strewn pathway with a raised eyebrow.

"You just missed it," said Judge Ophelius. "Dr. Foozle here was demonstrating some of his latest concoctions."

"I am aware," the count answered tonelessly. He took out his golden pocket watch, glanced at it, and put it back. "That's why I waited in the background until it was over."

The three men went up to the front porch of the mansion. Count Baines rang the doorbell. As they waited, Count Baines murmured to the other two, "Think wisely about whether to continue. In approximately"—he glanced at his pocket watch again—"ten minutes, we won't have the option of leaving."

"What do you mean?" Dr. Foozle blinked behind his spectacles.

Count Baines did not answer. Wormwood opened the door.

"Perfectly punctual," the caretaker said. "The hosts are expecting you."

Chapter Eight

FOUR HOURS UNTIL MIDNIGHT

At most parties, the hosts would greet you at the door when you arrive. They might shake your hand, thank you for coming, and say with a big smile, "We're so glad you could make it!"

At the Amadeuses' household that night, however, the hosts were nowhere to be found.

"Oh crows, where are they?" said Mrs. Raven, checking the doorway now and then for the hosts to appear.

"I suppose it's not too unusual for the hosts to be late to their own party...."

"Not *proper* parties," said Duchess von Pelt, scandalized.

The guests had gathered in the dining hall. Each person was surprised at this year's turnout. There were only nine guests in total.

"Not quite how I remember the last event," Chaucer said with a smile. "But no matter! Sometimes a small party is just as much fun as a big one. Mmm, I wonder if Mort Amadeus is serving his famous pumpkin bread today."

"I thought it's just Maribelle and Edie hosting today," said Judge Ophelius, looking perplexed.

"Why?" Chaucer asked curiously. "Did something happen to Mort?"

Nobody answered. Everyone seemed just as confused as the next person. There were far fewer decorations in the room than at the Amadeuses' previous events—in fact, there were none. It was as if the guests had simply stepped into a house whose owners had forgotten they were arriving.

Wormwood placed a platter of teacups on the dining

table. Dewey, who had managed to sneak back into the dining hall unnoticed, picked up one of the small porcelain cups. It made a *clink* noise as it tapped the tray. He'd read somewhere that the brittle material was composed of bone ash and clay.

"Bones are supposed to contain magical properties, aren't they, Dad?" he said.

His dad was busy chatting with the other guests.

"I remember you from the last party! And you. And you!" Chaucer was beaming at everyone in the room. "I remember all of you! Wait, I don't think we've met," he added to Mr. H and Ms. H.

"Good evening," they replied. Both of them had, in fact, met Chaucer at the last party, but neither bothered to mention it.

The guests mingled. They chatted, laughed politely at jokes, and shared tidbits of their daily lives. Wormwood passed through the group, awkwardly balancing a silver tray of finger foods on his arm. The guests pretended to enjoy the snacks, even though the chips were stale and the apple slices tasted old and bland. *Things really have gone downhill in the Amadeus residence,* a few of them thought.

When Wormwood passed Dr. Foozle, the two made eye contact. Dr. Foozle reached inside his lab coat, but Wormwood murmured, "Keep it; we'll need it later tonight." The caretaker moved onto the next guest before a confused Dr. Foozle could ask what he meant.

Meanwhile, Dewey sat at the table, nibbling an old pumpkin chip, watching Wormwood warily. His attention was pulled away when Count Baines seated himself across from Dewey.

The tall, gaunt man looked bored. Dewey smiled to be polite, but the count merely raised his eyebrow. "Nice goggles," he remarked.

Dewey wasn't sure if the man was being sarcastic or not. He took off his copper goggles and wiped them on his shirt, embarrassed.

"These parties aren't usually for children," Count Baines said, glancing at his pocket watch.

"My dad brought me along," Dewey answered. "I didn't *want* to come."

The count gave him a wry look. "I don't blame you. The last time someone brought a child along, there was a . . . problem."

Dewey's heart thumped. "Was her name Beatrice Willoughby?"

The count's eyes widened slightly before settling back into their bored expression. "You know about it? Doesn't surprise me. Nearly everyone and their cat knows about it nowadays."

"So who *is* Beatrice Willoughby?"

Count Baines didn't speak for a moment. When he did, his voice dripped with contempt. "The Willoughbys are a powerful family," he said. "I've had the unfortunate experience of playing against Mayor Willoughby in a checkers tournament. Of course, if I had known that most of my winnings would be handed over to him in what's called the Winner's Tax, I never would have played."

"The 'Winner's Tax'?" repeated Dewey.

"The winner pays the loser ninety-nine percent of their prize money," the count replied. "Mayor Willoughby drafted the rule as soon as he lost the game. I took it quite personally, even after all these years—"

"The mayor is a sore loser," said Mr. H, startling the boy and the count. They had not noticed the cobbler standing nearby. He started to turn away but saw Dewey staring. "Oh, I guess we haven't met. I'm Mr. H.

This is Ms. H." The man nodded at the woman next to him.

Dewey blinked at the duo. He guessed they were in their forties—or maybe twenties? It was hard to tell because their features were so vague. (Then again, it was always sort of hard to tell ages with grown-ups.) "Hi, I'm Dewey O'Connor," he said, putting his goggles back on.

"A pleasure to meet you." Mr. H waved awkwardly. "Er . . . you're not from around here, are you?"

Usually when people asked Dewey and his dad this question, it was with an air of hostility. But Mr. H seemed nice enough, even if he wasn't the greatest at conversations.

"No, my dad and I travel a lot," Dewey said. "We've been traveling since I was a toddler."

The Hs didn't say anything but seemed impressed, and Dewey went on to add, "We've lived in thirty different places in the last six months." Now the Hs stared open-mouthed at him.

"That is incredible," said Ms. H. "How do you go to school?"

"I study on my own," Dewey said. "Everything I need to know, I learn from books." Even though Dewey loved visiting local libraries on his travels, he had always been curious about what a real school was like, being in a classroom with other students. It sounded fun.

"How old are you?"

"Eleven."

"Ms. H is the town schoolteacher," said Mr. H. "Her students range from six to sixteen years old."

Dewey's eyes grew wide. "Do you—do you think I can check out the school? My dad says I make a great scholar."

"Absolutely," said Mr. H.

"An ardent learner, hmm?" said Ms. H, frowning a little. "Yes, I suppose you can enroll in my school."

"Really? I'd love to! But...I don't know how long we're staying in town. My dad and I don't stay more than a few weeks in any given place."

"Is that so?" A relieved smile spread across Ms. H's face. "That is perfectly fine. Come by. We're starting our lesson on smoke and mirrors on Monday."

Dewey glanced across the room, where Chaucer was talking animatedly about a restaurant they had visited. Certainly, his dad wouldn't mind if he went to school for a day.

"Sounds great," Dewey agreed.

Count Baines yawned audibly. This conversation, like most things, was boring him. "Is it true that teachers keep apples on their desks?" he asked indifferently.

"Yes, it's a tradition from the 1700s," answered Dewey, who was well-read on many subjects. "Families used to be too poor to pay their teachers money, so they would bring in baskets of apples as payment. Nowadays, they're a token of appreciation."

Before they could continue the conversation, Wormwood announced from the front of the room, "Ladies and gentlemen, I have a message from your hosts, the Amadeuses."

A hush fell over the dining hall. Wormwood took out a folded sheet of paper. "I have been instructed to read this once the party is underway." The caretaker unfolded the paper and began.

Dear esteemed guests,

Thank you for coming to our party this evening. We regret that we have not been able to host our annual All Hallows' Eve event for the last twelve years. It has been difficult for our family because of the Incident. As you've probably noticed, this is a smaller gathering than normal. You are likely wondering why you've been invited.

Each one of you has been invited here for a reason.

Thirteen years ago, in this very house, one of you took the life of Beatrice Willoughby.

The room let out a collective gasp. A few guests murmured among themselves. Some looked around nervously. Others looked outright angry.

"Are they suggesting one of us is a criminal?" demanded Duchess von Pelt.

"But Mort Amadeus was arrested for the crime," Mr. H spoke up. "Surely he wouldn't be behind bars if he was innocent . . . ?"

Wormwood ignored them and read on.

Because that heinous person got away with it, the wrong person was accused. Mort Amadeus is serving a prison sentence while the real culprit runs free.

Tonight, we will make our case for Mort's innocence. Tonight, we will deal swift justice.

And by "we," we mean you.

You, dear guests, will serve as a jury. You must consider the evidence presented to you, follow wherever it leads, and help us identify the real culprit before midnight, which, according to the laws of Nevermore, is when the statute of limitations for such a crime ends. If that time comes before you succeed, the responsible party will run free forever.

The exits have been sealed. No one will be able to enter or leave the premises until then. Wormwood will provide you the first clue.

Thank you for your cooperation.

Warm regards,
Mort and Maribelle Amadeus

Chapter Nine

THREE HOURS AND FORTY-FIVE MINUTES UNTIL MIDNIGHT

Wormwood tucked away the piece of paper and faced the baffled guests. Nobody moved or spoke.

Chaucer was the first to break the silence. "What an unusual party theme!" he said in an upbeat tone. "Sounds like it will be . . . what's the word? *Fun!*"

Nobody else shared that sentiment. "Is this a joke?" sputtered Mr. H.

"Preposterous!" agreed Dr. Foozle.

"If one of us is a criminal—a *murderer*—shouldn't we call the police?" said Mrs. Raven worriedly.

One of the guests took out his cell phone, only to realize there was no signal in the Inkwoods. Others pressed the caretaker for more information.

Wormwood offered no explanation. "I am merely the messenger," he said.

He's lying, thought Dewey, remembering the conversation he had overheard between Wormwood and Maribelle.

"Are we really not allowed to leave until the party's over?" asked Ms. H. Another guest called out that it was against the law to keep someone in a place against their will.

"You must stay on the premises for the full duration of the party," Wormwood answered. "Leaving early would mean you're breaking your contract and make you subject to arrest."

"Arrest?" shrieked Duchess von Pelt.

"What contract?" Judge Ophelius demanded.

"It was written on the backs of your invitations," Wormwood replied.

None of the guests remembered reading any such

thing. Mrs. Raven reached into her shawl and pulled out her invitation. The back was blank. Mr. H took out his to examine as well. Again, nothing.

Wormwood grabbed Mr. H's invitation and inspected it for a few moments. The caretaker then muttered, "Aha!" before rummaging in his pocket and fishing out a match. After he lit the match, he held the flame to the back of the invitation.

The paper crackled, but the flame did not burn through the page. Instead, dark burn marks snaked across the paper in the form of a message.

"Potassium nitrate ink," Dewey whispered as he and the other guests stared at the cursive writing. "You can use it to write secret messages that are invisible to the eye."

They read the words that had appeared.

> *By RSVPing yes, you hereby agree to follow all instructions given at the party. This is a binding contract. Any violation will result in criminal arrest.*

"But if the writing was invisible, surely that nullifies the contract?" cried Duchess von Pelt.

The people turned to Judge Ophelius, who was, of course, the most experienced with legal matters. The judge cleared his throat and admitted, "I am not a big fan of invisible contracts myself. But a while back, Mayor Willoughby passed a law that deemed them legal in order to sneak in extra loopholes for a deal he was making. Considering this message on the invitation was there the whole time, and written within the boundaries of Nevermore, it is indeed legal and binding. You will, in fact, face charges if you try to leave."

The guests began arguing among themselves.

"Ah, I'm not staying to play some nonsensical murder mystery game against my will," scoffed Dr. Foozle, reaching inside his coat. Dewey thought he saw the pharmacist take out a tiny vial of white, glittery powder, but when he moved to get a closer look, Dr. Foozle abruptly closed his fingers and turned away.

"Not to mention there's apparently a kidnapper or murderer in the house," said Ms. H crisply.

Judge Ophelius, who was used to bringing an unruly court to order, pounded his walking cane on the wooden floor like a gavel. There was a somber silence.

"First of all, everyone is innocent until proven guilty,"

Judge Ophelius stated. "Furthermore, if this is an elaborate prank, which I assume it is, then it's an extremely distasteful one."

"It's not a prank, Your Honor," said Wormwood. "The person responsible for Beatrice Willoughby's disappearance is still at large and must be brought to justice."

Judge Ophelius squinted at Wormwood, whose face was still hidden beneath his scarf and top hat. *Odd he never takes them off*, the judge thought.

"Where are the hosts? May I have a word with them?"

"Mort is still in prison, Your Honor, as you well know," Wormwood answered, his voice slightly sharp. "And Maribelle will not be coming down to join the party until the very end. For all intents and purposes, *I* am your host tonight. Oh, that reminds me." He produced a sealed envelope and held it out to the guests. "The first clue," he said.

Duchess von Pelt took it suspiciously. She unsealed the ivory-colored envelope, then shrieked again.

Inside was a lock of hair.

The hair was medium-length and golden brown. "This is Beatrice Willoughby's hair," Wormwood explained to the flabbergasted guests. "It is the only piece of evidence the detectives recovered from the night she disappeared. I took the liberty of...ahem, *borrowing* it from the police station's evidence locker for the evening."

Chaucer had a puzzled look on his face. "Can someone please fill me in on this Beatrice Willoughby thing?" he asked. "Her name sounds vaguely familiar."

The others glanced at one another. There was another tense silence.

"Beatrice Willoughby was the Nevermore mayor's daughter," Judge Ophelius said finally. "She came here thirteen years ago with her father for the Amadeuses' annual All Hallows' Eve party. At some point during the evening, she disappeared and did not return by the end of the night."

"Yes, yes, I remember now!" said Chaucer, snapping his fingers. "She was dressed up in a princess costume that evening, wasn't she?"

Duchess von Pelt also recalled the little girl's costume. A lot of people had admired Beatrice's diamond-studded shoes and plain pink dress, even though it had been nothing like the royal gowns that real princesses wore. The duchess should know—*she* had been to balls with actual kings and queens.

Chaucer looked around at the guests with wide eyes. "You mean . . . Beatrice Willoughby went missing that night and was never found?"

"Yes, poor thing," murmured Mrs. Raven. Beatrice had never been one of those pesky kids who smeared gum on her porch. Although, there *was* that one time when Beatrice had infuriated the innkeeper, for an entirely different reason. . . .

Duchess von Pelt raised her chin. "You should know I have an airtight alibi for that night," she announced. "I was talking to *many* people the evening of the party. Ask any of them."

"Sounds like what a guilty person would say," Count Baines muttered under his breath.

Judge Ophelius continued the story. "Nobody saw Beatrice leave the house," he said. "The police were summoned, and investigators searched the place high and low. They've even searched the hidden passageways of the house, the tunnels that lead to various rooms behind the walls. The process took a long time. In the end, a decision was made to arrest Mort Amadeus, the head of the household."

Some of the guests nodded. Dewey, however, was

confused. "Arrested based on what?" he asked. "The lock of hair?"

"Dewey, don't be rude!" scolded Chaucer. He apologized to Judge Ophelius, "Sorry about my son, he's just a kid."

Meanwhile, the other adults in the room were wondering the same thing Dewey had asked. But they stared ahead confidently the way grown-ups sometimes do when they don't want to appear ignorant.

Only Wormwood said approvingly, "An excellent question. I am also curious, Your Honor, about how the decision was made."

Judge Ophelius pressed his lips into a thin line. "You don't have to keep addressing me as 'Your Honor,'" he said. After all, they were not in a courtroom, despite the strange fact that the hosts had mentioned the word *jury* in the letter.

The guests were still waiting for his answer. The judge felt his throat go dry. He avoided their gazes. *Well, the truth was going to come out sooner or later,* he thought.

Finally, he said, "Mayor Willoughby is a very influential man. After his daughter went missing, he was understandably upset. The loss of a child is extremely difficult to bear. He demanded immediate justice—or else, he reassured me, I would never preside over another case in this town again. Despite the lack of evidence, I was forced to give a quick verdict. Technically, Mort *was* negligent for having an unsafe house where a kid can disappear. . . ."

"But that is not the same as saying he was the *culprit*," clarified Wormwood.

Judge Ophelius lowered his head. "It's a moment in my career I was not proud of. That is why, since that day onward, I've promised myself to do better in upholding every case to the highest letter of the law."

There was a pause. The guests digested the judge's words.

Mr. H said, "So you're saying there is a good chance that Mort Amadeus *is* innocent?"

Judge Ophelius nodded.

"But why are *we* the suspects?" Duchess von Pelt snapped. "Anyone at the party thirteen years ago could have been responsible for her disappearance!"

"Plus, what's the point of having *us* solve this case?" added Dr. Foozle. "Shouldn't you get the authorities involved?"

"The case was already considered closed," said Judge Ophelius. "If someone wants to reopen it, there is a lengthy appeals process to go through in the court system. In addition, because the event happened thirteen years ago, there is a limited window of time left in which we can continue to file criminal charges. The statute of limitations, in other words."

"Statue?" said Chaucer quizzically. "Like a marble statue, sculpted by a sculptor?"

"Statu*te*, Dad" whispered Dewey. "It's another word for 'law.'"

"That's correct," said Judge Ophelius. "Statutes vary across different parts of the world. In this town, the statute of limitations for disappearances is exactly thirteen years."

Ms. H pursed her lips. "Why do crimes expire, anyway? Seems unjust."

"That is because over time, evidence often gets lost or destroyed," explained the judge. "Witnesses no longer remember certain facts that took place. It's the fairest way to keep things accountable in the justice system."

"So Beatrice Willoughby's perpetrators have until

midnight of tonight before they're off the hook forever?" said Chaucer.

"Precisely."

Dewey squirmed. He and his dad had picked the worst year to come to the party. "We don't have to stay here, Dad," he whispered to Chaucer. "We didn't get an invitation, so we aren't bound by the contract. We should leave."

"Don't be ridiculous!" Chaucer replied loudly. "Since we're already here, we might as well make the most of it!"

"We do have a lot of time left," spoke up Mrs. Raven, glancing timidly at the grandfather clock in the corner of the room. "I suppose we can't do much else.... The contract forbids us from leaving until midnight...."

The others did not reply. Wormwood remained as unhelpful as before, but he seemed to smile behind his scarf. "I am certain if you work together, you will find the culprit."

Work together? The guests protested. Were they really expected to work together when there was a possible murderer-slash-kidnapper among them? Worse, what if the murderer struck again?

"We would be safer if we stayed together," said

Mrs. Raven. "The culprit wouldn't do anything in front of all these witnesses."

That made sense. Some of the guests relaxed, but just a tinge.

"And recall, if you will," Judge Ophelius reminded everyone, "that there was no proof anyone was even murdered, as Beatrice's body had never been found." He turned to Wormwood, looking annoyed. "Now, I am curious about the wording of the hosts' letter. . . ."

As the judge pestered the caretaker, Dewey thought about the conversation he had overheard earlier upstairs. He decided he would tell his dad about it later, when nobody else was listening. After all, he wasn't sure which guests he could trust yet, and right now Chaucer seemed eager to talk to *everyone*.

"The clock is ticking." The caretaker waved away the judge and stood tall, a trace of amusement in his voice. "Let the party *officially* begin."

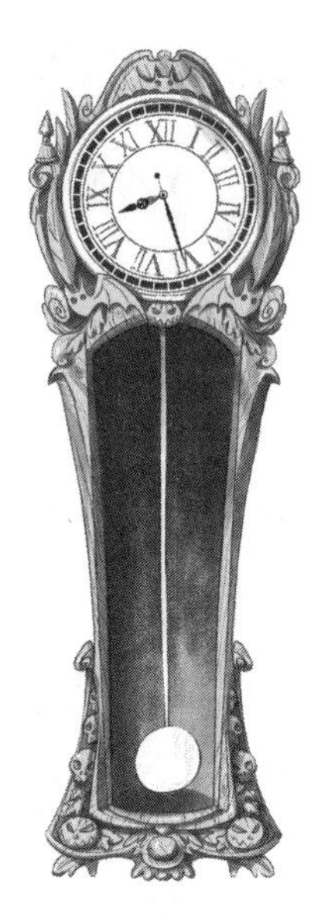

Chapter Ten

THREE AND A HALF HOURS UNTIL MIDNIGHT

The guests began studying the first clue. Duchess von Pelt was the first to make a guess. ("I am excellent at solving my daily crossword puzzles," she told everyone. "My butler helps me no more than half the time.")

The duchess held up the lock of hair to the fireplace, examining it in the orange light. "Perhaps it indicates that Beatrice Willoughby was balding," she suggested.

"Ah, alopecia," said Dr. Foozle. "It's a condition that makes people lose their hair."

"*Did* Beatrice have alopecia?" Chaucer asked.

Another person said they should contact the mayor to confirm.

"We are not calling Mayor Willoughby at this late an hour to ask about his missing daughter's hair," declared Judge Ophelius.

Dewey turned to Wormwood and asked, "Where was the lock of hair found?"

"Another excellent question," said Wormwood. Dewey blushed. "It was found in the game room. This way, please."

The game room was down the hallway. Every inch of the space was occupied with miscellaneous toys and games: dolls, dice, poker chips, paddle boards without the string, board game pieces, yo-yos, paddle boards without the ball. There were several billiards tables and multiple dartboards.

Overlooking all the games and toys was a foreboding

painting of Mort. He wore a somber expression, as if he disapproved of games and fun. It was a rather odd piece of decor, given the purpose of the room.

"They could use a better interior decorator," remarked Duchess von Pelt.

"The lock of hair was found under that chess table over there," said Wormwood, ignoring the duchess.

The guests sidestepped the clutter and looked around. Meanwhile, Dewey quietly turned to a blank page in his book, a giddy feeling in his stomach. He considered himself a decent detective. He had read every original Sherlock Holmes novel and every mystery by Agatha Christie, and he had learned a few tricks of the trade. A disappearance in a mansion? It was a classic case.

The first rule of being a detective, he knew, was to be observant. He took out his trusty pocket pencil and began to write down notes.

SUSPECTS

Suspect 1: Mrs. Raven

Innkeeper of Nevermore Inn. Smiles at everyone nervously.

Suspect 2: Duchess von Pelt

Loud and opinionated, kind of annoying. Dress has fresh flowers sewn onto it.

Count Baines picked up a chess set, looking bored. "There weren't any fingerprints collected from this room?" he asked.

"There were too many guests coming and going that night," said Judge Ophelius. "It would have been useless to collect all of them." Knowing the others were depending on him to take charge, the judge added, "But perhaps we can look for some now. Fingerprints can last quite a while on surfaces."

Suspect 3: Judge Ophelius

Judge. Solemn and logical. Carries a lot of guilt about the past.

"Unfortunately, everything has been cleaned in the last ten years," said Wormwood.

"Not cleaned well," remarked Count Baines as nearby, Dr. Foozle picked up a dusty Scrabble box and sneezed.

Suspect 4: Count Baines

Disinterested in everything, it seems.

Suspect 5: Dr. Foozle

Pharmacist. Keeps checking the inside of his lab coat.

"Excuse me, but what was Beatrice like?" asked Dewey.

The adults in the room didn't answer right away. The question seemed to make them uncomfortable.

Dr. Foozle spoke up first. He chose his words carefully. "Beatrice Willoughby was an . . . *inquisitive* child," he said, adjusting his spectacles. "She would ask me all sorts of questions about the potions I sell in my pharmacy. One time I caught her watching me through my shop window—" He paused. It would be doubly incriminating if he mentioned that Beatrice saw him brewing something highly illegal.

"She once tried to take a crow home from my inn," spoke up Mrs. Raven, her pale cheeks suddenly flushed. "Said she wanted to set the crow free. I told her to leave the bird alone immediately. Later, Mayor Willoughby sent me an angry note, and I was forced to pay a fine for disagreeing with his child."

"She was six," said Wormwood flatly. "All kids at that age love animals."

"Of course," said Mrs. Raven quickly. "I wasn't faulting her for that. . . ."

Dewey did not think Beatrice sounded like a bad kid. She seemed curious, just like him. Wormwood apparently agreed, because he made a *tsk* noise and added, "Listen to you all, acting high and mighty. I don't know of a single human child who's perfect. To be frank, I don't know of a single human *adult* who's perfect."

"Speak for yourself," said Duchess von Pelt, smoothing the petals on her dress.

Mrs. Raven examined the lock of hair again. "Oh crows!" she suddenly exclaimed. "It looks like it was cut off, based on the edges—see how it's angled?"

The guests circled around and took a closer look.

"You're right," said Judge Ophelius.

"I wonder why anyone would choose to cut off a lock of her hair?" said Ms. H.

"Ah, this doesn't answer your question, but bone and hair *do* make up the basic composition of all humans, along with skin," said Dr. Foozle. "Hair is important because it contains a person's unique DNA. In ancient times, it was often thought that having a lock of a person's hair would give you control over them."

Mrs. Raven shivered and said, "That reminds me of part of a spooky poem I once encountered: *To a rag and a bone and a hank of hair, we called her the woman who did not care.*"

Chaucer asked Dr. Foozle, "What happens if someone's... what's the word? *Bald.*"

"Beard or armpit hair work fine, too," said the pharmacist.

Chaucer scratched his red beard, then clapped his hands excitedly. "This reminds me of the story of the scientist who tried to bring a human back to life!" he said. "Do you remember that one, Dewey?" He pulled out his notebook again and looked through the pages. "Aha! Here it is."

Once upon a time, in the mountains of central Europe, there was a brilliant scientist. He had created many marvelous inventions. He made potions for staying awake, elixirs for making you laugh, brews for cleaning the inside of your nose so you never have to pick it again.

"I'm not sure this is the best use of our time," interrupted Judge Ophelius.

Dr. Foozle was watching Chaucer with a strange expression on his face. "No, please keep reading," he insisted.

Chaucer continued to read.

But he wanted to build the ultimate creation: a living, breathing adult human, made from scratch.

The scientist spent years holed up in his laboratory, working long days and nights on his project. He used old body parts dug up from graves and magical potions to glue the pieces together.

What resulted was a frightening mess of a creature, not quite human but not quite an animal. It was a mishmash of old skin and hair and bone, a reanimated corpse. But it was empty, soulless, hollow. It turned on its creator and killed many of his loved ones before vanishing into the mountains, never to be seen again.

"Oh crows," murmured Mrs. Raven, clutching her chest.

"How macabre," agreed Ms. H, using one of her favorite spelling words.

"Grave digging is illegal," Judge Ophelius reminded everyone sternly, just in case anyone got any ideas.

"Ah, the story is probably nothing more than an urban legend." Dr. Foozle cleared his throat, his cheeks suddenly red. "But if the scientist is real," he added in a rush, "he's certainly *not* me, or my grandfather's great-granduncle for that matter.... Definitely not someone I know of...."

The others gave the pharmacist a peculiar look. *What's that simpleton rambling about?* thought Count Baines, before glancing at his pocket watch and promptly losing interest.

"So it's possible to re-create a human from old skeletons?" Chaucer asked excitedly.

"*No,*" answered Dr. Foozle. "The point of the experiment is that we *can't*. Despite the basic chemical breakdown of our bodies, we aren't just made of bones and hair and skin. There's a spark of magic that everyone has, from the moment we're born. Some call it our soul.

Nobody has figured out how to re-create that spark yet. Only take it away."

Dewey, who was jotting down the pharmacist's words, set aside his pencil. "How would someone take away another person's spark?" he asked.

"Well, killing them is the most obvious way," said Dr. Foozle. "Then the spark leaves and floats away like a leaf. However ... it is also possible to steal the spark and *preserve* it using a spell, locking it inside a box of some sort."

"What, like a safety-deposit box?" asked Count Baines with a bored sneer.

"Could be, I suppose. I'm sure you could use just about anything as a vessel, as long as you keep an eye on it."

"And what happens to its original owner?" one of the guests asked.

"They'd be a hollow puppet, like in the story," said Dr. Foozle. The pharmacist looked thoughtfully into the distance and murmured to himself, "Ah, that's what old Victor should've done.... He should've reanimated the corpse with a *true* human spark.... Then the disaster that ensued might have been entirely avoided...." He trailed off after seeing most of the guests were looking at him strangely again.

"We're getting off-topic," said Judge Ophelius, stepping in. "Let's look at the facts. All we know is that Beatrice had been in this room, and that someone cut off a piece of her hair."

"Was anyone here *with* Beatrice at any point during the party?" asked Ms. H.

Several guests shook their heads. Count Baines stiffened, then ducked his head and looked intently at his pocket watch. Duchess von Pelt pursed her lips and pretended to adjust her dress petals.

Dewey had an idea. "We should figure out which other rooms in the house she had been in," he suggested.

Judge Ophelius answered that the mansion had been full of guests, and that people had been flitting from room to room like moths. "She could've been in any of the rooms," the judge said. "And like the caretaker said before, all footprints and fingerprints would have been cleaned away by now."

"What about using a hound dog? They can track scents."

"Investigators have already searched the place with

their best hounds," stated Judge Ophelius. "Nothing unusual has been found on these premises, aside from the lock of hair."

"It's not about finding things but figuring out where in the house Beatrice has been," pointed out Dewey. "It could tell us important information, like what she had been doing before she disappeared."

The judge shook his head. "Even so, I cannot obtain a hound dog from the police station on such short notice."

Dr. Foozle adjusted his spectacles. "Have you considered using a *specter* hound?" he suggested.

"What's that?" asked Dewey, who had read about all kinds of animals, including axolotls and platypuses, but had never heard of a specter hound.

"Regular hounds sniff a crime scene in order to find a person's body using their scent. A specter hound does the same thing, except instead of smelling the person's scent, it tracks down the person's *essence*."

"Their essence?" one of the guests said dubiously. "You mean the person's spark you just spoke of?"

"In a sense," explained Dr. Foozle. "People leave imprints of their spark all the time. Like footprints, except they never disappear. It happens when the person puts a bit of themselves into something. It can be a hobby they enjoy immensely, or it can be something they create, like a piece of artwork they drew or a poem they wrote."

"So my essence would be in the dresses I design?" asked Duchess von Pelt.

"And mine in the pies I make?" asked Mrs. Raven.

"And mine in the shoes I fashion?" spoke up Mr. H.

"Yes, yes, and yes," said Dr. Foozle. "A specter hound can track down someone's essence easily, because a specter hound itself is made of spirit material."

Judge Ophelius raised his eyebrow. "And how do we create these so-called phantom hound creatures?" he asked skeptically.

Dr. Foozle hesitated. Should he tell them? No, it was a waste of precious bone dust. Yet across the game room, Wormwood was watching him knowingly—and, when the others weren't looking, gave the pharmacist a slight tilt of the head. This must be the reason for bringing the bone dust, Dr. Foozle realized. Again, it was proof the caretaker was in on the night's shenanigans. As long as Dr. Foozle obeyed, nothing bad should happen to *him*, right? In fact, it might even clear his name....

He slowly reached into his lab coat. Everyone in the room watched curiously as the pharmacist took out a tiny glistening vial of fine white dust. Dewey's mind raced; he recognized the vial from earlier.

"As a matter of fact, I can create a specter hound. I'll need to use a sprinkle of this bo—this perfectly legal magical substance," Dr. Foozle quickly corrected himself, giving Judge Ophelius a nervous glance. "I'll also need a piece of cooked meat and a tennis ball."

"A tennis ball?" repeated the guests.

"All dogs love tennis balls," said Dr. Foozle with a shrug. "It's part of their essence." He cleared his throat. "In addition, because the contents of this vial are very rare, I'll need, um, compensation."

Compensation? He wants us to pay in a situation like this? Outrageous. The others wrinkled their eyebrows. Wormwood leaned forward and appeared to start to say something but stopped. Dr. Foozle had hypothesized correctly that the caretaker would not mention the money that the Amadeuses had already paid the pharmacist—not in front of the judge.

Instead, Wormwood made a *tsk* noise behind his scarf and muttered, "Greedy humans."

Judge Ophelius reached into his wallet. It did occur to the judge that Dr. Foozle was one of the suspects, but they needed to move things along. "If it aids the investigation, then so be it," he said, and placed some money in Dr. Foozle's hand.

"Excellent," said Dr. Foozle, closing his fingers around the cash. "Now we just need to find a tennis ball and a piece of meat."

After digging through the game room, one of the guests found an old tennis ball lying at the bottom of a basket. Wormwood left the room and came back a moment later with a piece of leftover sausage. Dr. Foozle took the two items in his hand, uncorked the vial of bone dust, and sprinkled some of the fine powder over the whole thing.

The bright powder shimmered, emitting an eerie white glow the color of moonlight. Moments later, the powder began to float like dust particles in a sunny room. The particles slowly drifted onto the carpet. As they did, the bone dust multiplied. They formed tiny glittering lumps that looked first like a dog's paws, then a dog's body, until finally, the sparkling dust settled into what was unmistakably a small dog with a wagging tail. It raised its long nose and floppy ears at the guests.

None of the others had seen such a thing.

"Unbelievable," breathed Judge Ophelius as the specter hound barked noiselessly at his heel.

"At least it doesn't drool or leave fur everywhere," said Duchess von Pelt, who hated all animals.

Dr. Foozle took Beatrice's lock of hair and held it before the glittering, dusty creature. "By using Beatrice Willoughby's hair," he said to the dazzled guests, "the specter hound should be able to extract her essence."

The creature sniffed the lock of hair, then weaved through the room, stopping at various games and tables. It made no sound as it moved; rather, it was like a whispery shadow. The guests leaped and stumbled out of its way. As the dog brushed past them, they could feel a cold breeze where the specter hound had touched their skin.

"Ah, this must be one of the items that Beatrice enjoyed," said Dr. Foozle as the specter hound lingered near the chess set.

The phantom creature sniffed the room once more, then bolted out the door.

Chapter Eleven

THREE HOURS AND FIFTEEN MINUTES UNTIL MIDNIGHT

The specter hound trailed down the hallway and up the stairs. The guests followed the phantom dog hesitantly, unwillingly. No one really wanted to see where it was leading them (except Chaucer, who gawked at the corridors like he was at an amusement park). But they didn't have a choice.

The house was quiet, save for the guests' creaky steps and quiet conversations.

"I really wish you told me about the existence of specter hounds thirteen years ago, Doctor," Judge Ophelius murmured. "It would have helped the Willoughby case immensely."

"Ah, well, I wasn't involved in the investigation," responded Dr. Foozle. "Besides, like I said, the substance used to make a specter hound is illeg—I mean, very, very rare."

Near the back of the group, Dewey looked over the guest list in his book. He had forgotten to write down the last two suspects. It took him a while to remember their names.

Suspect 6: Ms. H
Schoolteacher. No description.

Suspect 7: Mr. H
Town cobbler. No description.

Are Mr. and Ms. H married? Dewey pondered. Or were they merely siblings? They looked practically identical, that was for sure. He closed his book and rushed to catch up to his dad.

"There's something I need to tell you," Dewey whispered.

"Isn't this party fascinating, Dewey?" Chaucer said brightly. "I've always wondered what it's like to be a... what's the word? *Investigator!*"

"Dad, I overheard something before the party," Dewey tried again. "The caretaker is in on the whole thing."

"That nice fellow, Wormwood? But he told us he didn't know what was going on. He said he's just the messenger."

"Trust me, he's lying—"

"Your goggles look dirty," Mrs. Raven said next to them, interrupting their conversation. Dewey blinked at the innkeeper, who grimaced disapprovingly and offered, "I can clean them for you if you'd like."

"Uh, no, that's okay." Dewey explained the goggles were made of copper and were supposed to be reddish-brown. "They help me read in the dark."

Mrs. Raven scrunched up her dark eyebrows. "Why would you want to do that?"

Dewey found it an odd question. "Because sometimes there's a book I haven't finished reading, and it's past my bedtime," he explained. "I put these on so I can read under the covers."

The old woman gave Dewey a closer look. "Oh crows, you are a clever child, aren't you?" she said, more to herself. "Yes, indeed..."

Up near the front of the group, Count Baines took out his pocket watch. He didn't see the person next to him and bumped into her, nearly dropping the watch.

Count Baines said irritably, "Watch it—" What was the woman's name again?

Ms. H merely nodded and returned a rueful smile. She was used to people forgetting her presence.

"Beatrice Willoughby was in your class, right?" Wormwood said from behind them.

The schoolteacher squinted at Wormwood. Was there something deliberate in the caretaker's innocent remark, or had she imagined it? "Yes, Beatrice was," answered Ms. H cautiously. "She was a... standout student, always eager to know more."

"That's the best kind of pupil, isn't it?"

"She certainly left an impression in the classroom, yes." The persistent caretaker was almost as exhausting as Beatrice had been, and Ms. H was relieved when Wormwood's gaze fell on the count.

"That's a nice watch you've got there, Count Baines," Wormwood said. "By the way, I'm surprised *you* don't know who the culprit is."

The count stiffened. Now it was his turn to eye the caretaker suspiciously. "Why would I know that?" he replied slowly.

Wormwood did not respond, his expression hidden underneath his scarf and top hat. Count Baines became flustered—*he* was usually the one who refused to answer other people's questions (with a sense of smugness, he might admit).

"Watch your step in fifty-five seconds," he said aloud to the group as they went up the narrow staircase.

About a minute later, the specter hound paused on the second landing, where it seemed to have lost focus and doubled back to circle the guests' feet. Startled, Duchess von Pelt almost tripped near the banister, breaking the heel of her shoe in the process. Mr. H apologized and said she could get a discount on her next pair of shoes, while Dr. Foozle spent several minutes mending the heel with one of his sticky glue potions, after reassurances from the duchess that she would pay him after the party.

"Dogs love to chew on shoes in real life," Dr. Foozle tried to explain to the amused cobbler, as the specter hound paused to yap soundlessly at Mr. H's boots before trying to nibble at his ankles. The pharmacist scolded the creature. "Focus! You have a job to do."

The specter hound folded its tail between its legs shamefully. After the interruption, they followed the hound to one of the doors, where the creature opened its mouth and barked silently. Wormwood opened the door.

"This is Mort's study," said Wormwood. "It hasn't been used since he was arrested."

He went inside the dark room and lit a reading lamp. The others followed him. Inside the room was a wooden writing desk and bookshelves with glass cases. Enclosed in these cases were not books, but hundreds of marionettes. There were puppets of all kinds, each dressed up in a different outfit. There was one of a baker, dressed in white and carrying a rolling pin.

There was a puppet of a mountaineer with breeches and a black hiking vest. There was even one of a mortician—it held a black book with a cross, standing next to a mini coffin. The guests stared at the collection in amazement.

"These belong to his wife, Maribelle," said Wormwood.

"Yes, we know," said Chaucer. "I recall she's an excellent puppet maker! I didn't manage to purchase a souvenir at the last party, to my everlasting regret. . . ."

"Maybe today you can," said Mrs. Raven.

"Doubt it," muttered Count Baines.

Dewey blinked for several moments at a puppet that bore a strange similarity to Chaucer, from the bushy red beard right down to the blue notebook Dewey's dad often carried. Before he could point this out, the specter hound ran up to the desk and made a barking motion.

"It detects Beatrice's essence in here," explained Dr. Foozle, following the creature across the room to the desk. "She must have been here at some point during the party."

Cluttered on the desk were several mundane things—paper clips, fountain pens. The specter hound motioned to the desk drawer with its nose. Dr. Foozle opened it to reveal a notepad. He picked it up. A cloud of dust made him sneeze.

"That desk hasn't been touched since the Incident," said Wormwood.

"I can see that." Dr. Foozle scrunched his nose uncomfortably and sneezed again.

"Oh, let me." Duchess von Pelt, who never sneezed in public, reached for the notepad and started skimming through the pages. Her eyes widened beneath her veil, and she leaned closer.

"What?" demanded Judge Ophelius. He took the notepad from Duchess von Pelt and looked through it. His eyebrows rose.

On the pages were black-and-white pen drawings, the kind of doodles a young, inexperienced artist might make. There were three pictures. Each one contained what looked like a smiling princess. There was one drawing of the princess playing chess with a tall, frowning man. There was another of her talking to a bird. Handwritten at the bottom of each picture was *Beatrice Willoughby,* and underneath that, the date—October 31, exactly thirteen years ago.

"Beatrice Willoughby must have drawn these the night of the party," said Judge Ophelius in a low voice.

The guests gathered around the judge and looked at the drawings. A shiver crept down their backs. They couldn't explain why, but the doodles were... *unsettling,* like seeing a doll with rotting teeth.

The last picture in particular stood out. It was a doodle of the princess with a woman in a dress. The woman's face was scribbled out.

Judge Ophelius gripped his walking cane. "I'm surprised the investigators never bothered to examine this notepad," he commented. His voice was quiet and troubled.

"Is it a clue, Your Honor?" asked Wormwood.

"It may very well be one. If the art imitates life, then it shows who Beatrice interacted with the night of the party."

There was a chess set in the game room, remembered Dewey. Beatrice Willoughby must have been playing chess with one of the guests....

Count Baines's mouth tightened, his frown matching the one on the man in the drawing. "It doesn't mean those people portrayed in the notepad are guilty," he pointed out.

"You are correct, Count Baines," agreed Judge Ophelius. He took the notepad and placed it in a pocket within his robes. "However, it does mean that whoever they are, they have moved up on our list of suspects."

Chapter Twelve

THREE HOURS UNTIL MIDNIGHT

The grandfather clock in the dining hall downstairs chimed nine. The sound swept across the floorboards and through the walls.

Upstairs, the specter hound jumped off the desk and snuffled out of the study. The group followed the phantom dog down the hallway again.

This time, the creature led them to a door at the end of the hall. The door was locked.

"Huh," said Wormwood. "Nobody has been to this room in ages." The caretaker fished in his pockets and took out what looked like a long, thin skeleton key. He twisted the key into the lock and opened the door.

The inside looked like some sort of sitting room. There were dozens of chairs of all kinds: folding chairs, armchairs, wooden stools, leather sofas. All of the seats were dusty from disuse. Cobwebs dangled from the furniture and the corners of the walls. The flowery wallpaper was faded, and a single candle sat on the sconce in the dim room, lighting itself as soon as the door had opened. (*Not a bad idea to have self-lighting candles in a giant mansion,* Dewey realized. *Otherwise it takes forever to tend to each candle.*) Soft music played from an enchanted pianoforte next to the window.

"This used to be Mort's mother's room," said Wormwood. "She now prefers the attic. Please, have a seat."

Some of the guests sat down in the dusty chairs. Others refused and stood awkwardly.

The specter hound circled the room and stopped in front of the thick window curtains. It began to jump and bark noiselessly again.

"It found something," reported Dr. Foozle.

Mrs. Raven opened half of the curtains. They seemed rather useless, seeing as how the outside of the window was pitch-black day and night. *But curtains are good for privacy,* Mrs. Raven supposed. She pushed aside the other half of the curtains, then gasped.

A scarecrow stared back at her in front of the glass.

It was a small scarecrow, half the size of a regular one you might see on a farm or in a cornfield. The head was made of tweed fabric, with black buttons sewn for the eyes and a crooked stitch for the mouth. The rest of its straw body was stuffed into a pink gown. A rusty silver tiara rested on top of the scarecrow's scraggly yarn hair. The whole thing seemed oddly menacing and out of place.

"Ah, that's...strange," said Dr. Foozle. It was an understatement.

"I agree," said Count Baines in a monotone. "The point of a scarecrow is to scare away birds *outdoors.* It serves little purpose indoors."

Dr. Foozle watched the phantom dog jump and yap noiselessly. "What's stranger is the specter hound seems to indicate that the scarecrow contains a very strong dose of Beatrice Willoughby's essence."

Judge Ophelius stepped forward. "How long has this scarecrow been here?" he demanded.

Wormwood tilted his head and shrugged. "We stopped using this room after Edie moved out," he replied. "That was thirteen years ago. Some of this stuff could have been here for ages."

Judge Ophelius said nothing. He took out the notepad from earlier and glanced at the drawings, then back at the scarecrow. His gaze lingered on the tiara.

The guests read the judge's ashen expression. Mrs. Raven clutched her chest. "Are you thinking that the scarecrow is . . . ?" she murmured.

"That can't be Beatrice Willoughby," Mr. H said, his face devoid of expression as he inspected the inanimate, smiling object. But he sounded uneasy.

Judge Ophelius glared at Wormwood. "None of the files for the case mentioned a scarecrow," he said. "However, I am certain those are the same dress and tiara Beatrice Willoughby wore the night of the party."

The silence that followed was thick and stifling. It was the kind of pause that came right before something big happened, a lull before the storm.

Chaucer sat forward on a sofa and tapped his beard

thoughtfully. "You know, this reminds me of the tale of the Scarecrow Children."

Dewey swallowed a groan. "Not now, Dad," he whispered.

"No, no, I think this story is quite appropriate. I recall hearing this one when we passed through Lower Saxony up in Germany. Do you remember, Dewey?" Chaucer hurriedly flipped through his notebook again. When he found the page, he began reading.

Once upon a time, there was a faraway town that experienced a mysterious phenomenon. Every so often, the townspeople would wake up and discover a scarecrow perched on their front porches.

Nobody knew where the scarecrows came from. The scarecrows wore different outfits—winter jackets, sundresses, even bright swimsuits. There was something familiar about the expressions each scarecrow wore, but the townspeople couldn't put their fingers on what.

Then one night, a local boy named Timmy Weber sleepwalked out of his house. He was still in his pajamas, half dreaming, with no awareness of what he was doing.

The next morning, after discovering him missing from his bed, Timmy's frantic parents ran outside to find their son. There was no trace of him. But there was a scarecrow perched on their front porch.

Suddenly, the mother shrieked, "That scarecrow is wearing the same pajama set Timmy wore last night to bed!"

"Sorry," said Chaucer sheepishly after he realized the jaws gaping at him around the room. Even the pianoforte had stopped playing. "Got carried away there."

"So you're saying the *children* got turned into scarecrows?" clarified Duchess von Pelt.

"Yes, that seems to be the case, or so the story goes," Chaucer said lightly. "Odd, isn't it?" He straightened on his sofa and admitted, "It might not mean anything in this instance, of course. . . ."

But the minds of the other guests were already humming with this new piece of information, which obviously did mean something. "How exactly does someone turn a child into a scarecrow?" Ms. H demanded.

Dewey stood up straight. It just so happened that he had asked the exact same question when he'd first heard the story from his dad many years ago. He had gone to a local library during their travels and researched all he could about enchanted scarecrows.

"It's an ancient magic," he said. "It doesn't have to be kids. Anyone can be turned into a scarecrow. It's the same way you can stitch people into puppets and dolls. You would need something from the person—a lock of hair, for instance—and a cursed spinning wheel."

"A cursed *spinning wheel?*" said Duchess von Pelt, laughing. "What kind of ridiculous thing is that?"

Dewey's cheeks flushed. "I don't know how it works, exactly. From what I've read, the spindle has to be enchanted with a particular spell."

"I've heard of such things," said Judge Ophelius without smiling. "There was that famous court case of a young woman in France who pricked her finger on a cursed spindle, then fell into a deep slumber for eighty years."

"Did she wake up old and wrinkly?" said Ms. H, sounding slightly horrified.

"No, she looked exactly the same as before," the judge answered. "I believe, in that case, the spell was a kind of magic that preserves your body so it doesn't change at all, similar to a stone or a painting. I assume the same thing happened with the children who got turned into scarecrows."

Nobody spoke. Magic was at the foundation of their lives, in everything from blooming flowers to warts on the back of a toad. But it was understood that what mattered was what a person *did* with magic. Because some kinds of magic went against what nature intended. Turning kids into inanimate objects was one of them—something only the most wicked, evil person would do.

The guests blinked at all that was left of Beatrice Willoughby, at her lifeless smile and fabric skin and button eyes. Several of them shuddered. *What a terrible way to die.*

"*Is* she dead, though?" pointed out Dewey.

"My guess is that the body will not die unless its

spark of magic fades," theorized Dr. Foozle, adjusting his spectacles. He started to say more, but Duchess von Pelt cut him off.

"You are all overthinking this," she scoffed, crossing her arms. "Frankly, this seems like a forgotten piece of decoration to me. The Amadeuses probably used it at one of their previous All Hallows' Eve parties."

"We did not," Wormwood replied.

Judge Ophelius stooped closer to the scarecrow. "It *does* look like a piece of decor," he agreed after a moment. "That's probably why the authorities didn't bring this in as evidence." He turned to face Wormwood. "You say Mort's mother hasn't been in this room in ages?"

"Yes, Your Honor. She moved to the attic shortly after the Incident."

Count Baines looked at his pocket watch with a bored expression. "Perhaps someone should check under the scarecrow's left foot," he suggested. When the others looked at him questioningly, he added, "No need for me to explain, one of you will do what I say soon enough."

Dewey was the one who finally reached forward and lifted the scarecrow's leg. His eyes widened. Wedged between the rough straw was a folded note.

The inside read, in the same cursive writing as the invisible contract,

Search the place where dishes sit,
Where you can save a banana split.
Look closely and you will find
Something cold for a fowl mind.

"First an oddly placed scarecrow, now an oddly placed riddle?" said Dr. Foozle, adjusting his spectacles.

"Less odd than intentional," Count Baines corrected.

There was no doubt now that the evening's events had been carefully planned, like acts in a play. The guests rounded on Wormwood.

The caretaker shrugged one shoulder and said calmly, "I was only given instructions about the lock of hair. I know nothing more about anything else."

Does he think we're simpletons? thought Count Baines, his lips curled into an amused smirk. He sat back on a wooden chair, then noticed the others were now eyeing *him* suspiciously.

"How'd you know the note was hidden there, Count Baines?" asked Judge Ophelius.

The count rolled his eyes. "I predict things," he said simply.

Several of the guests looked amazed. Others, who'd crossed his path over the years, only nodded. *That's right, I forgot about his ability,* thought Judge Ophelius, recalling the time the count warned him about a crooked lawyer who would bring fake evidence into the courtroom.

"You mean you can see the future?" asked Chaucer, bouncing eagerly. "Can you tell me if I'll ever win the lottery?"

"Better yet, what are the winning lottery numbers for next week?" someone else chimed in.

Simpletons. Count Baines sighed in annoyance and said, "The farther out the event is, the hazier it is to predict. I cannot see what happens in a week, or even in a few days. I can, however, predict things that will happen in the next few minutes with absolute clarity."

Next few minutes? The guests frowned. That seemed like a useless ability. They could simply wait a few minutes and see what happened themselves.

Duchess von Pelt's voice was more high-pitched than usual. "So you . . . *can't* predict who the real culprit is?" she asked. "Is that right?"

"The prediction has to contain some indication that the person is the culprit," Count Baines replied. "A sign of some sort, whether by their actions or another person's. For instance, if I see a vision of someone getting hauled away in handcuffs tonight, then we can deduce that person is the culprit."

"Oh crows, *does* anyone get arrested?" Mrs. Raven asked, wringing her hands.

The count shrugged. "I do not know yet."

The guests murmured in disappointment. "We'll have to wait until Count Baines makes a new prediction," said Judge Ophelius.

"You'll let us know immediately once you figure it out?" Duchess von Pelt pressed, looming over the count.

"Yes, yes, you'll be the first to know," the count muttered in a tone that implied the exact opposite.

"All right," said Judge Ophelius, drawing everyone's attention to the task at hand. He nodded at the piece of paper that Dewey held. "For now, it appears we have a riddle to solve."

They read the piece of paper again.

Chaucer clapped his hands. "It's like a...what's the phrase? *Scavenger hunt!*"

"The clue is in the kitchen," declared Duchess von Pelt confidently. "*Where dishes sit,* and *Where one can save a banana split.* Those are things that belong in a kitchen." She was proud that she'd come up with the answer by herself.

"They can also be in a dining hall," pointed out Mrs. Raven. "It's the one other place in the house where you eat things."

"In our caravan, the bedroom doubles as the dining room," chimed in Chaucer.

"Right, well," Duchess von Pelt said, irritated at being corrected. "You can check those places if you want. *I'm* going to the kitchen."

"I vote we stick together in case someone tries something funny," Count Baines said in his monotone.

"Safety in numbers," agreed Mrs. Raven.

With that, the guests headed back downstairs to the kitchen.

At previous parties, the Amadeus kitchen had been full of noise and clutter—steaming pans, salad spinners, and harried cooks running about in white mushroom-shaped hats. The air would be filled with the aroma of roasted vegetables and stews and rich desserts, and the guests would crowd around the doorway, mesmerized and licking their lips.

Now the kitchen looked like it hadn't been used in ages. The floor was dirty. Grime coated the stovetop. Unused pots sat in a cluttered heap on the counter, covered in stains and dust.

"Huh, that explains the sad state of the snacks earlier," muttered Count Baines.

Chaucer went to examine several dusty containers of herbs. "So, what are we looking for?" he asked, picking up a jar of shriveled basil leaves.

"We have to find *something cold for a fowl mind,*" recited Mrs. Raven.

"A foul mind," repeated Dr. Foozle. "We're looking for something a repulsive person would enjoy?"

"Like rotting cabbage?" asked Mr. H.

"Or mayonnaise," someone else suggested with a shudder.

"Not *foul* mind, darling," Duchess von Pelt corrected. "*Fowl,* as in birds. It seems we must look for something that birds enjoy."

Dewey frowned. He didn't think that was what the riddle meant exactly, but the others had already started digging through the kitchen for things like seeds and worms. They peered inside the oven. They searched inside the cabinets. They looked inside every cup and glass. The specter hound weaved through the kitchen, sniffing silently in corners and giving what looked unmistakably like a sneeze.

"Do birds like maple syrup?" said Chaucer after examining a half-used bottle of maple syrup he'd pulled from one of the shelves.

"Not particularly," answered Mrs. Raven.

A thought occurred to Dewey. The clue mentioned banana splits. Banana splits were kept *frozen*. His heart leaping, he glanced around the room. His excitement dwindled. Oddly enough, there was no refrigerator in the kitchen, let alone a freezer.

"Um, where's the . . . ?" Dewey paused. None of the grown-ups were paying attention to him, except Wormwood beside the door.

The caretaker turned his head, his face still hidden in the shadows of his hat and scarf. "Where's what?" Wormwood inquired.

"There's no refrigerator, is there?" said Dewey.

"Very observant. No, there is not."

Dewey was puzzled. Even his dad's caravan had a mini-fridge, a clunky and used one that they had picked up from a yard sale. It seemed odd that a mansion as lavish as the Amadeuses' didn't have one.

Mrs. Raven, who had overheard the two, said, "How in the world do people survive without a fridge?"

Dewey remembered reading about life before the refrigerator was invented. "People lived without them for centuries," he said. "You preserve foods by pickling or salting them, or drying them out, like jerky. You can also store vegetables and fruits in cellars, where it's often cool and dark."

Wormwood rolled his head. "Yes, that is exactly right." *At least one of them has a brain,* the caretaker thought. *The plan just might work....*

"Is there a cellar in this house?" asked Judge Ophelius, putting down a dusty saltshaker.

"Right this way, Your Honor."

Chapter Thirteen

TWO HOURS AND THIRTY MINUTES UNTIL MIDNIGHT

The group descended into the cellar. ("I knew the clue referred to the cellar; it was quite obvious," Duchess von Pelt said loudly.) That part of the mansion smelled damp, like the ground after a rainstorm. It was also colder. Shivering slightly, the group headed down the narrow stone passageway, their path illuminated by the duchess's floral lantern.

Wormwood stopped in front of a heavy wooden

door half the height of most of the guests. He pushed it open with a soft grunt. The inside was pitch-black.

"Oh crows, I don't like this," murmured Mrs. Raven as she stooped down to crawl inside the short entryway.

The others followed suit. Suddenly, Chaucer let out a yelp. "I saw something!" he cried.

He bumped into Wormwood, who bumped into Dr. Foozle, who bumped into the person ahead of him, and so on. The group toppled like a row of dominoes. Luckily, the room was so cramped, they simply jostled against the stone wall instead of falling flat on their faces. Dewey, who saw things clearly with his lit-up goggles, was the only one who avoided the chaos.

It turned out the thing Chaucer had seen was the specter hound, who panted happily. "It's too dark in here," Chaucer said apologetically to everyone. "I wish I had my flashlight with me."

"Ah, I believe I have some spare sunlight left." Dr. Foozle took out a glistening bottle from his lab coat. He adjusted his spectacles and examined it. "Alas, there's very little left... and it is rather difficult to replace..."

"I'll pay you," Chaucer said eagerly.

"Oh?"

"I have a bunch of stuff back in the caravan I can trade."

"I suppose that's acceptable." Dr. Foozle uncorked the bottle. A moment later, floating orbs of sunshine danced in the air and lit up the darkest corners of the room, which in any other setting looked more like a dungeon. The light revealed the trunks and barrels that lined the dark walls.

Wormwood explained that this was where the Amadeuses stored their perishable goods. The guests examined the barrels, revealing batches of onions, potatoes, and dried meat.

"But the clue mentioned '*where dishes sit*,'" said Mr. H after a few moments. "There are no plates or bowls here."

"Dishes can mean plates *or* the food served in them," piped up Dewey. He stood off to the side, trying to avoid bumping into the others in the cramped space.

As he took a step back, he brushed against a wooden box near the corner. It was ice cold. Dewey jolted. *A literal icebox!* He had read about such things. Back before the invention of refrigerators, ice was a luxury, and people kept it in wooden boxes, like cold treasure chests.

Slowly, Dewey opened the lid. Frozen air greeted him. When he looked inside, his eyes nearly popped out of his head.

"What do you have here?" said Mrs. Raven behind him.

Before Dewey could speak, a loud gasp came from the innkeeper. Mrs. Raven gave a small cry of recognition.

"Oh crows!"

She was exactly right. At the bottom of the box was a dead crow.

The others gathered around the icebox to take a peek. "Well, it's certainly for both a fowl mind . . . and a *foul* mind," remarked Count Baines dryly.

Most of the guests kept their distance from the dead bird. Ms. H excused herself and stepped out of the room. Duchess von Pelt maintained her composure, but she kept her veiled face turned away. Dr. Foozle rubbed his spectacles. Count Baines glanced at his pocket watch. Even the specter hound barked noiselessly and scurried out of the cellar.

Only Mrs. Raven picked up the bird. An unreadable expression passed over her face. "Poor fellow," she said softly.

The others waited. Everyone in town knew how much Mrs. Raven liked black birds. The Nevermore Inn was full of stuffed dead crows, some resting, others poised as if taking flight midair. Several people who had stayed at the Nevermore Inn claimed to have heard Mrs. Raven conversing with the crows, debating about the best types of cleaning supplies and the best trees to build nests in. (But those might just have been rumors.)

Not everyone shared the innkeeper's admiration for fowl creatures, however.

"Get rid of it, please," Duchess von Pelt ordered, pinching her nose so that her voice sounded nasally. "Dead animals stink horribly."

"I don't smell anything," Dewey said.

"The poor fellow's been dead for years," said Mrs. Raven. "Usually birds decompose within a week, given how small they are. But because of the ice, the body seems to have been preserved rather well." She examined the crow in her hands. Again, that unreadable look from before passed over her. "He's thirteen and a half years old," she added.

"How can you tell?" someone asked.

Mrs. Raven's lips tightened. "I just can."

Count Baines shrugged indifferently. "Nothing we can do about it now. The crow's dead."

Chaucer asked if the crow had been a cherished pet of the Amadeuses.

"The Amadeuses do not keep *pets*," Wormwood said indignantly, spitting the word as if it had a bad taste. "*Pet* implies humans are the master, and animals serve no master unless they are being paid."

Mrs. Raven gently lifted the bird's stiff wing. She examined the crow's feathers and felt its cold, lifeless claws. *You've done well, old friend,* the innkeeper thought. She knew what she would do: she'd take the bird back to the Nevermore Inn. She would mount him next to the other crows, keep him company. Maybe she'd have this one crouch near the service desk and keep a watchful beady eye on the customers, especially mischievous children who liked to climb all over the furniture.

Judge Ophelius rounded on Wormwood and demanded, "What is the meaning of this?"

"You keep asking me to explain things, Your Honor, but I don't know any more than you," Wormwood replied. "I am merely the caretaker."

"An icebox is no place to keep a bird," Judge Ophelius stated. "At least, not in my experience."

"Maybe the bird crawled into the icebox by itself," said Wormwood, sounding rather amused. "With all due respect, this place is huge. We have all sorts of random spiders and rodents and bugs living in the walls. Am I now responsible for explaining *those*, too?"

"Preposterous!" Dr. Foozle said. "The bird was obviously planted, as was the poem."

Several others grumbled in agreement.

"Maybe the bird is a spy," suggested Chaucer, his eyes shining. "Like in the story of the Magpie Spy." When the others stared at him blankly, he said, "You've never heard of the Magpie Spy?"

The others shook their heads. Chaucer excitedly opened his notebook to find the page.

There once was a pie maker who worked for a powerful king. The pie maker was excellent at making pies. Any type of pie you can think of, the pie maker could make. Apple pies, pumpkin pies, blueberry pies, banana cream pies.

Every day, the pie maker prepared a fresh pie

for the king's afternoon meeting, which was when he discussed important, secret matters with his advisers. The king never ended up eating the pies. The pies were there simply to make the meeting room smell good.

One day, however, the king was hungry, so he sliced open his pie. When he did, something weird happened. To his surprise, a black bird popped out and began to sing.

He called for the pie maker to be brought before him. "What is this dish you have set before your king?" he boomed.

The pie maker replied calmly, "Your Majesty, it's a magpie, of course!"

It turned out the pie maker had baked birds into the pies in order to spy on the king's secrets. The king tried to arrest the pie maker, but the bird pecked out the king's eyes before he could. The pie maker escaped, never to be seen again.

"Magpies are a type of bird from the same family that crows and ravens come from," Dewey informed the confused guests.

Mrs. Raven smiled nervously at Chaucer. "W-where'd you hear that story?"

"*I've* heard the story before," cut in Duchess von Pelt. "The von Pelts have connections to all the powerful families in the world. The pie maker must be old now, wherever he is."

"Yes . . . *he*," Mrs. Raven mumbled. She quickly cleared her throat and stroked the bird gently. "However, it's true that crows can make excellent pies—I mean, spies. They have exceptional memories."

They all peered at the dead crow again.

"Well, *this* one's not remembering a thing now, and I say it's nothing but an All Hallows' Eve prop, just like that scarecrow upstairs," insisted Duchess von Pelt, still holding her nose. She turned and headed for the door. "This is ridiculous. I'm leaving."

One by one, the others slowly followed suit. But Mrs. Raven stayed where she was. She glanced over her shoulders. When she thought no one was looking, she gently pressed the bird's beak.

"What are you doing?" said Mr. H, who had remained behind.

The old woman froze. She had not noticed the cobbler standing next to her. "Oh, nothing, I just thought I'd . . . um . . ." Seeing no way out, she sighed and confessed, "I thought I'd heal this bird."

The others stopped at the doorway and stared at Mrs. Raven. "Ah, but the bird's already *dead*," repeated Dr. Foozle slowly.

But even before the pharmacist finished his sentence, the crow's small head twitched. Its wings started to shake. The others gawked, stunned. The bird's eyes fluttered open.

"What the—?" gasped Duchess von Pelt.

The crow let out a cheerful caw.

"You can . . . raise crows from the dead?" Judge Ophelius said to Mrs. Raven. He blinked at the humble old woman, not quite sure what to make of her.

Mrs. Raven sighed. "I don't tell people this often, but I come from a line of necrowmancers."

"What?"

"Necrowmancers. Crow healers. It's not a particularly useful skill, not something you use every day." Mrs.

Raven quickly added, "I don't use it *often,* oh crows, no. Only in emergencies. If a crow had a particularly short life, for instance...hit by a car, or electrocuted in a thunderstorm..."

The reawakened crow cawed several times. It ascended through the air, flapping its black wings, renewed with vigor.

Incredible, the guests thought. They looked closely at the innkeeper—was she working together with the Amadeuses?

"The crow could have been a witness the night of the party," Dewey piped up. "Bringing it back to life might be, um, useful...." His voice trailed off in embarrassment.

"Surely you jest," Duchess von Pelt laughed loudly. "How can a *bird* be a witness?"

"Actually, there have been cases where animals testified in court," said Judge Ophelius. "There was a case where a dog had witnessed a house break-in. The court brought it before a row of suspects, and it barked at the one it recognized."

"Animals are quite clever," said Wormwood, a proud note in his voice.

Mrs. Raven stroked the bird's wing. The crow made a friendly noise.

"Yes, I know," Mrs. Raven cooed. "It's been a while, hasn't it?"

The crow tilted its head and cawed again.

"Are you going to fill us in on what's happening?" said Ms. H, who had reappeared in the room. "We can't all speak to birds like you do."

"Oh crows, oh yes," Mrs. Raven apologized, blushing. "He came here with someone thirteen years ago for the party. Apparently, he had been hiding out in the mansion by himself, clever bird. Then a few years after the party—he doesn't remember the exact number, since the Inkwoods stay dark day and night—he got caught." There was an edge to the innkeeper's voice, and she added bitterly, "He tried to escape but flew into some loose puppet strings. I presume that's when he got placed in the icebox."

Again Judge Ophelius glanced warily at Wormwood.

"Don't look at me, Your Honor," the caretaker responded.

Birds do not simply go undetected inside houses, the judge started to say, but his gaze shifted to Chaucer, and he closed his mouth.

"Does the crow know anything about Beatrice Willoughby?" pressed Dewey.

Mrs. Raven and the crow conversed in a series of squawks and caws. The innkeeper didn't speak for a few moments.

"What is it?" someone called out.

"He said…he saw someone lure a girl in a princess gown away from the party.…He saw them go upstairs.…When they emerged, Beatrice wasn't with them. She had been turned into the"—Mrs. Raven's voice trembled—"the *scarecrow*."

The cellar had gone deathly still. Each of the guests stared at Mrs. Raven, some of their mouths hanging open.

Chaucer jumped and said excitedly, "See? It's just like the story!"

"Who was it?" Judge Ophelius asked the crow in a stern voice. "Was it someone in this room?"

The crow carefully tilted its head to study each guest with a beady eye. The room became so quiet, nobody seemed to breathe. An uneasy thought crossed Dewey's mind—*what if the bird remembered wrong?* He had read about countless people throughout history who had been imprisoned after being falsely accused. When the crow turned to stare at him, Dewey's heart lurched.

The crow cawed again. Mrs. Raven shook her head. "He doesn't remember," she translated.

The guests slumped their shoulders in disappointment (or perhaps it was relief). "Hardly surprising," muttered Count Baines, wiping his forehead. "It happened so long ago."

Mrs. Raven, however, was puzzled. Crows were extremely smart creatures; they rarely forgot a face. Dewey, who had read the same thing in an encyclopedia, suggested, "Maybe the person was wearing a disguise."

"None of the adults wore disguises that night," Wormwood confirmed. "The parties have a strict dress code . . . unless you're the daughter of the mayor, in which case we grant exceptions unwillingly."

"Well, *I* hardly think a crow is fit to be a witness," Duchess von Pelt said, her face hidden behind her veil.

"Nevertheless, we should alert the authorities and inform them what the crow witnessed," said Judge Ophelius. He turned to Wormwood. "Is there a working phone in this house?"

"Doesn't matter," the caretaker said gruffly. "There's no time to get the police involved in a formal investigation, Your Honor. In a few hours, the statute of limitations expires." Wormwood took a deep breath. "Once that happens, there's nothing more that can be done."

Chapter Fourteen

TWO HOURS UNTIL MIDNIGHT

Upstairs, the clock chimed ten. Two more hours until midnight.

Duchess von Pelt declared she couldn't stay in the cramped cellar anymore ("It's suffocating, darlings, and I have a sensitive nose"). The guests went back upstairs to the dining hall. After drinking some tea, they sat in a daze around the table, mopping their brows. Most of them were still shaken by the night's turn of events.

A talking crow, an enchanted scarecrow... They had no idea what to make of it.

Such awful hosts, they agreed. Weird, strange hosts with an odd sense of humor.

Mrs. Raven gulped down her fifth cup of tea, wishing she could be back in her warm, cozy inn. She fed a pumpkin chip to the crow perched on her shoulder. "How awful," she murmured. She wouldn't enchant a kid into a scarecrow, no matter how mischievous the child was—well, unless the child knocked over one of her treasured mounted crows in the Nevermore Inn. *That* would be unacceptable....

Chaucer glanced around the table. "I've been told there have been multiple kids who've disappeared in this town," he said. "At least one a year, close to All Hallows' Eve."

"Yes, the town has had an unusual pattern of missing children," said Count Baines, looking up from his pocket watch to peer at Chaucer closely. He had thought that the traveling storyteller was nothing but a simpleton, yet he seemed to know quite a lot about what went on....

"It's nothing to be worried about," said Duchess

von Pelt as she brushed cookie crumbs off her gloves. Next to her, the specter hound tried to eagerly lap up the crumbs that fell to the floor, but they merely went through its tongue as if it were air. The duchess wrinkled her nose at the creature and scooted her chair away. "They probably just get lost in these dreadful woods," she added.

"The Inkwoods are not a maze," replied Wormwood, his voice hard. "If children have gotten lost in the woods, eventually they would have found their way out."

"Unless they were taken by someone inside these woods," pointed out Dr. Foozle as he adjusted his spectacles.

"Are you suggesting the Amadeuses kidnapped the children?" Wormwood challenged.

The duchess waved him off. "One of them was *arrested* for the Beatrice Willoughby disappearance, darling," she replied airily. "Even if Mort's somehow innocent, he and the rest of his family are prime suspects."

Tap-tap-tap. Judge Ophelius rapped his walking cane, putting a stop to the bickering. "Enough with these mindless accusations. We do not know whether the culprit responsible for Beatrice Willoughby's disappearance is the same person behind these other missing children."

"If that were the case, then there would probably be random scarecrows of the missing children around town, right?" said Chaucer as he helped himself to a pumpkin chip.

Several of the guests exchanged furtive glances. "But scarecrows are common around town, especially in autumn," said Ms. H slowly.

"They're traditional All Hallows' Eve decorations," agreed Mrs. Raven, biting her lips nervously. "Nothing unusual in that."

The guests thought of the harmless scarecrows they'd encountered over the years, out in the fields or perched at the end of the odd lane, half-hidden in shadow. Could they have been the imprints of the missing children?

In the corner of the room, Dewey was quietly jotting down notes. He was in a bad mood. Earlier, on the way to the dining hall, he had finally managed to tell his dad about the conversation between Maribelle and Wormwood, but Chaucer simply dismissed his suspicions that something bigger was afoot. *"Not now, son. I have to interview Mrs. Raven about her crow-talking abilities!"*

Under the entry for Mrs. Raven, Dewey added,

> *Likes birds a lot. Would likely be an expert on scarecrows.*

He studied his notes. There were many unanswered questions. The events of the night kept getting stranger and stranger. Dewey closed his eyes in thought and mumbled to himself.

"Why, what?" said Wormwood.

Dewey looked up, startled. He hadn't realized anyone was listening. He closed his book and said, "I, um, was just wondering why anyone would kidnap a child every year. It's almost as if there's a *schedule* to it."

Judge Ophelius overheard him. "Certain kinds of magic are like that," said the judge. "They rely on cycles, like the full moon."

"Magic that runs on a strict, regimented schedule is almost always health-related," added Dr. Foozle. "My customers tend to require weekly or monthly potions."

"You mean like medicine?" said Mrs. Raven.

"Ah, precisely. Taking one vitamin a day, for instance."

"So whoever's kidnapping one child a year might be doing it for . . . health reasons?" Dewey was skeptical.

Wormwood echoed Dewey's skepticism. "If *only* there was a place we could research the answers to such questions," the caretaker mused.

The word *research* clicked in Dewey's mind like a flashlight. He turned to Wormwood. "What time does the Nevermore public library close?" he asked, right before realizing the silliness of his question. None of the guests could leave the house that night.

But the caretaker's answer was unexpected. "The town's library is pitiful," sniffed Wormwood. "It only has things that Mayor Willoughby likes to read. If you want to see a *real* collection of rare, wonderful books, the Amadeuses have a nice library of their own down the hall."

"Really?" spoke Judge Ophelius, his face lit up. "I am quite fond of good books myself."

"A lover of books, are you?" Chaucer said to the judge. "You and my son would get along. You are both . . . what's the word? *Bibliophiles.*"

"Yes, and I find books often hold the answers to puzzling questions," the judge answered pointedly. Dewey adjusted his goggles and nodded.

Judge Ophelius and Dewey followed Wormwood back down the corridor, the rest of the group lagging behind them begrudgingly. The caretaker stopped in front of a pair of dark doors that nearly blended into the wall. He fumbled for a key, then led them into the room.

Right away, Dewey and Judge Ophelius recognized the familiar, sweet smell of old books. The bookshelves were full of them, in all sizes and muted colors. A warm glow lit up the large fireplace in the corner. In front of it was a plush rocking chair, exactly the kind of chair you might use for sitting comfortably with a good novel. Behind the bookshelves, wide windows encased the Amadeus library, and the dark Inkwoods pressed in from three sides. If it weren't for the fact that the Inkwoods blotted out the sun, the library would have been a perfect place for reading during the day.

"Very nice," Judge Ophelius said admiringly.

"Certainly better decorated than the rest of the house," agreed Duchess von Pelt. Even she spoke in a quieter voice than usual. There was something about the library that made the guests want to hush and simply sit and ponder life's greatest questions.

The guests glanced at the titles on the shelves with interest. Wormwood had been right that the collection was intriguing. An old green tome titled *Frightening Flowers* caught Duchess von Pelt's eye. Count Baines raised his eyebrow at a book titled *101 Ways to Tame a Bat*.

Dewey scanned the spines. One black book, thick and embossed with fine gold thread, grabbed his attention: *Grimms' Tales*. The edge of the book stuck out over the shelf, as if someone had been reading it recently and only hastily put it back. He thought back to the earlier clues—the oddly placed scarecrow, the oddly placed riddle. *"Less odd than intentional,"* the count had said. With that, Dewey pulled the oddly placed book off the shelf. The worn pages were full of fables and familiar bedtime stories that Dewey recognized.

Wormwood nodded at the book. "The Grimm brothers were some of the greatest journalists," he said. "They interviewed folks about all sorts of... well, *grim* events across Europe. The stories became classics, I am told."

"Amazing!" said Chaucer. "Maybe one day my chronicles will be published in a book as well."

Mrs. Raven clutched her shawl and shivered. "I remember my mother telling me some of these stories. Scared the daylights out of me. There is one about two kids who got lost in these very Inkwoods more than a hundred years ago."

"Ah, my grandfather's great-granduncle met them," mentioned Dr. Foozle. "Apparently, they met an evil witch who wanted to eat their hearts. The witch locked them inside a house made of gingerbread. But they managed to escape by using a cunning plan to trick her."

Ms. H shook her head. "More likely they were just lucky," she murmured.

Dewey turned the pages. He wondered why witches and villains in stories always tried to lure kids away, instead of their parents. The tales were full of warnings about children who followed strangers and disappeared in the middle of the night. It was odd there were no such lessons for adults, because Dewey had met his fair share of clueless grown-ups who weren't that much smarter themselves.

As he examined the book, he noticed a felt ribbon

between two of the pages. He opened the book to where the ribbon lay. An illustration of a woman with her face hidden behind a handheld mirror greeted the reader. In the woman's other hand was squeezed what was unmistakably a human heart.

"Hmm, I remember reading this," said Judge Ophelius, seeing the familiar story over Dewey's shoulder. "Textbook case on how envy rots the human mind. The tale is widely known all over Europe—a girl who was the fairest and prettiest in the land, and the wicked stepmother jealous of her beauty. The stepmother ordered someone to kill the girl and bring back her heart."

The adults in the room tutted, muttering, *"How despicable."*

"Perhaps she had a good reason," said Duchess von Pelt, whose voice had gone slightly cold. "The stepmother might have gotten tired of hearing the girl prattle about her good looks all the time.... I can't imagine having to listen to someone so vain, can you?"

"Yes," said Count Baines shortly.

Judge Ophelius made a face at the duchess, then continued, "Yes, well... *luckily,* the stepdaughter was able to escape and hide in a den of goblins."

Wormwood made a *tsk* noise. "Why do so many people in these stories want human *hearts,* of all things?" he said with disgust.

Dr. Foozle slowly adjusted his spectacles. "Ah, the heart is said to be full of wonders," the pharmacist said. "Remember how I mentioned earlier that everybody is born with a spark of magic? That spark has been traced to the heart, which is the core of every human. Theoretically, there are all sorts of remedies you can extract from a human child's heart. It is pure and ripe with magic, ten times as much as a grown-up's."

"What kind of remedies can one make with a child's heart?" asked Chaucer curiously.

"Hypothetically, a child's heart is the perfect ingredient for anything that has to do with increasing your lifespan. Youth potions, longevity elixirs, anti-aging tonics . . ."

Elixirs and tonics? Several of the guests glanced sharply at Dr. Foozle. Could the pharmacist be the one who collected children's hearts once a year, soaking them in jars of chemicals?

As if reading their minds, he retorted, "The health board keeps a close eye on my potions and brews. I don't use any illegal ingredients, thank you very much!"

A few feet away, Judge Ophelius let out a chuckle, which he quickly disguised as a cough. *Does the pharmacist think none of us recognized the bone dust earlier?* he wondered. Under normal circumstances, he would have had Dr. Foozle arrested on the spot, but they had bigger problems right now. Besides, the specter hound had been quite helpful in tracking down the scarecrow. The judge held his tongue.

Breathing fast, Dewey closed his book with a thump, his own heart beating rapidly. "That must be it, then," he said. "Whoever's behind these disappearances is after the *child's heart*."

The guests blinked at the boy.

"That's horrible, stealing children's hearts just so someone else can live longer," Ms. H said.

"Eternal life has been sought after since the dawn of time," said Wormwood. "I'm sure many humans would *die* for the key to a long lifespan."

"So someone stitched Beatrice into a scarecrow... presumably to steal her heart." One of the guests glanced at Dewey. "Didn't you say earlier that such a wicked handiwork requires a cursed spinning wheel?"

Dewey blinked behind his goggles at the man, then

remembered his name was Mr. H. "That's what I've read," he said.

"Oh crows, the culprit must have used one on Beatrice Willoughby," Mrs. Raven fretted. The bird on her shoulder made a distressed noise.

Wormwood rolled his head. "I do not recall anyone carrying a spinning wheel to the party that evening," he said.

No, those are much too big and bulky, Dewey agreed. A spinning wheel wasn't like a book or a glass vial one could keep hidden in their jacket. "Do the Amadeuses own a spinning wheel?" he asked aloud.

The caretaker paused before answering. "As a matter of fact, they do," he said. "It has been in this household forever. . . . It belongs to Edie."

Most of the guests remembered Edie. She was very old and frail and hardly left her wheelchair. At every party the Amadeuses had hosted, she'd sat silently with her embroidery in her lap, her needle and thread in hand. If anyone asked her a question or tried to strike up conversation, she'd stitch out her answer with the thread.

As with the rest of the Amadeuses, nobody had seen Edie for thirteen years.

"Excellent seamstress," recalled Chaucer. "Mended my cloak at the last party after I accidentally ripped it. Looked good as new after. She can't be the culprit, she's too kind."

A couple others agreed that Edie was a nice old lady who couldn't possibly be responsible for such a terrible crime.

Judge Ophelius remembered Edie was one of the suspects who had been instantly cleared of suspicion in the Beatrice Willoughby case. "*The old woman can hardly walk,*" the investigators had said. "*There's no way she's involved in this.*" Perhaps they had been too hasty, the judge realized.

"We must consider all possibilities in order to narrow down the true culprit," he reminded everyone. "To do that, we must put aside any personal beliefs we might have about a person." He gripped his walking cane and stood up. "Wormwood, is Edie in the house right now?"

"Yes," Wormwood answered hesitantly. "She's in the attic, where she stays most of the day."

"Then the most immediate course of action is to question her about the spinning wheel."

Wormwood woodenly held up an arm. "I'm afraid

that's not possible, Your Honor," he said. "Edie refuses to talk to anyone who was at the last All Hallows' Eve party."

"Why?" asked Chaucer.

"Think about it," Wormwood replied. "She is convinced one of the guests at the party was responsible for the Beatrice Willoughby disappearance. Yet it was her own son who was arrested, with little to no evidence." Wormwood paused, then added dramatically, "None of you bothered to speak up for Mort's innocence at the time."

The caretaker turned to face each of the guests one by one behind his scarf and top hat. Mrs. Raven fidgeted. Duchess von Pelt made a scoffing noise. Count Baines avoided eye contact by glancing at his pocket watch.

"I am certain she would readily assist us," argued Judge Ophelius. "We're trying to prove Mort's innocence tonight."

Mrs. Raven stroked the crow on her shoulder and said softly, "No, it's true. The last time I saw Edie in town was thirteen years ago, just after Mort was arrested. I said hello, but she gave me an icy glare as if I had smacked her."

The others were skeptical. "You're telling us she can remember *every* single person who attended the party thirteen years ago?" said Count Baines, raising his eyebrow at the caretaker in disbelief.

"Edie may be old, but she's sharp as a tack," confirmed Wormwood. "She'd recognize every one of you."

Except me, thought Dewey, who hadn't been at the last party. But he did not mention this out loud. Predictably, the other grown-ups seemed to have overlooked him—just as they overlooked the two guests who continuously faded into the background. It was only after one of the two spoke up for a third time that the others, after exchanging momentary confused glances, recalled who they were.

"Good idea, Mr.—um—Mr. H," said Chaucer. "One of us could put on a mask to fool Edie!"

Wormwood made a scoffing noise. "Do you think Edie's an idiot? She wouldn't be deceived by a simple mask...although some of you could significantly improve your appearance by wearing one." He shrugged at the dirty looks several guests tossed him. "What? I'm just telling the truth."

"Oh, but it's not the outside that counts!" said

Chaucer. "Nobody enjoys a book with a rotten story inside, no matter how brilliant the cover. To judge something solely based on the exterior is...what's the word? *Misleading*."

"Why don't we simply have the caretaker himself talk to Edie?" Count Baines suggested, reading his pocket watch with a bored expression.

"I'm afraid that poses a conflict of interest," said Judge Ophelius firmly. "The two of them are practically family, and we want to be as impartial as possible. No offense," he added to Wormwood.

"None taken," the caretaker replied. "Edie will refuse to speak to me anyway if she knows it's to help the judge who sentenced her son to prison."

While the group continued to debate the best way to approach Edie, the two forgettable guests quietly retreated out to the empty hallway. Once they were alone, Mr. H made a face.

"This party definitely isn't what I expected," he said.

"Obviously, it's not what *any* of us expected, but never mind that now," said Ms. H. "Listen, I have an idea. The two of *us* should talk to Edie!"

"Us? Why?"

"Everyone always forgets our faces. I bet she doesn't remember us from the last party."

"That's true," agreed Mr. H. "But what's the point? Do you really think *Edie's* the right person?"

"Think about it." Ms. H glanced up and down the deserted corridor before lowering her voice. "The scarecrow in her room, the dead crow, the spinning wheel... The clues all point to her perfectly."

The Hs mirrored one another with a raised eyebrow. Each was thinking the same thing.

"Yes, the clues are certainly incriminating. In that case, Edie..." said Mr. H slowly.

"...is the culprit," Ms. H finished.

Chapter Fifteen

ONE HOUR AND FORTY-FIVE MINUTES UNTIL MIDNIGHT

Mr. and Ms. H slipped down the hallway and began their ascent up the staircase. They continued up past the second landing to the top floor and headed down a long, dark corridor. The floorboards up there were dustier and creakier, as if they hadn't been properly maintained in a while. Cobwebs clung to the corners of the ceiling. The two looked around cautiously, using the flickering candle that Ms. H had swiped from one of the walls downstairs. A lone spider sleeping in one of the cobwebs jumped at the newcomers, then disappeared inside a crack in the wall.

There was only one door, all the way at the end of the corridor. An embroidered doormat lay in front of the door. Usually, doormats said things like, WELCOME! or HOME SWEET HOME. Edie's read, in stark letters,

VISITORS UNWELCOME.

The Hs approached the door and knocked. There was no answer. They knocked again.

"Hello?" called Ms. H.

"Hello?" called Mr. H.

"Hello?" someone replied timidly behind them.

It was now the Hs' turn to jump, startled. They turned, wide-eyed. A pair of red, circular eyes greeted them in the dark corridor.

Dewey emerged, the goggles on his face glowing like lightbulbs. "I, um, thought I could come along and see what Edie says," he said.

After the two grown-ups got over their initial shock, they regarded the eleven-year-old for a couple seconds.

"Shouldn't you be with your dad?" said Ms. H. "I'm sure he's worried about you running around by yourself in a place like this, after what happened to Beatrice Willoughby."

"He's not worried," Dewey said flatly.

The Hs exchanged a glance. "This is a dangerous situation," Mr. H said to Dewey. "We don't want something bad to happen to you, too. Haven't you heard the saying '*Curiosity killed the cat*'?"

Dewey could tell they weren't altogether comfortable with having him tag along. He wanted to laugh out loud—he and his dad had been to far more dangerous places before, such as the grove they once stumbled upon that played eerie music anytime someone got close, or the bottomless bog that looked like a simple rain puddle from above. Still, it was awfully kind of the Hs to care about him.

Maybe he needed to demonstrate his usefulness. "I can take notes," he said. "Plus, I've read about cursed spinning wheels. I know how to tell them apart from regular spinning wheels."

"How's that?" asked Ms. H.

"If the spinning wheel is cursed, then the spindle has a reddish glow to it."

The two adults looked impressed. "Interesting," said Mr. H. "It'll be good to have someone knowledgeable like you along."

Ms. H's smile drooped slightly. Despite her aversion to clever children, she wasn't about to object aloud. The boy knew a lot—a suspicious amount, it seemed. She should keep an eye on him and his boisterous, storytelling father.

The Hs turned back to the door and knocked again. After another moment of silence, Mr. H tried the door handle. It was unlocked. Slowly, he opened the door.

Behind the door was a small enclosed space. There were no windows, and the air was stuffy and hot and smelled faintly of wet leaves. A single lantern glowed on a small nightstand. Like Edie's previous room, there were dozens of chairs and sofas scattered around the already cramped place, leaving barely enough room to walk.

An old woman sat in the far corner, in a red armchair that had stuffing spilling from the seams. Her back was turned to the guests, her snowy white hair barely visible over the back of her chair.

"Hello, Edie," Ms. H said. "We are guests here tonight, and we wanted to speak with you."

Edie did not answer.

The guests squeezed through the chairs and lounges to where she was sitting. Edie, they saw, was very, very old and very tiny. Her skin was papery thin and hung off her bony features. She wore a flimsy nightgown and was embroidering a pillow on her lap. Sewn on the pillow in tiny cursive writing were random phrases like *Fine, thank you,* or *One cup of coffee, no sugar.*

"Nice room you got here," Mr. H said unconvincingly.

Edie continued to embroider with her needle, her colorless, pale gray eyes staring straight ahead.

"We won't trouble you long," Ms. H said, clearing her throat. "We only wanted to ask you about the spinning wheel you own. You see, we are interested in the intricacies of... of thread-making."

Again, Edie said nothing.

"Maybe she can't hear us," Dewey whispered, lifting his goggles.

Then he saw it: a new message had been sewn on the pillow in blue thread.

I've haven't had visitors outside this family in thirteen years.

Dewey had never seen anyone sew that quickly.

Letters appeared on the pillow beneath every twitch of the needle. He nudged the Hs, and the three of them stared, mesmerized, at the words.

Did Wormwood let you in the house? I heard the doorbell ring earlier.

The guests nodded. "We're here for the All Hallows' Eve party," Mr. H said hesitantly. Edie's face darkened. "But . . . did you not know about it?"

New words appeared under the seamstress's flurry of fingers. *They did not tell me there was one tonight.*

Edie was no fool. Despite being in her mid-eighties, the old woman had an impeccable, sharp mind. She knew something strange was going on that evening. For one thing, Wormwood still hadn't brought up her evening tea. For another, he and Maribelle had been insistent that Edie remain in her room for the duration of the night . . . for different reasons. ("We're doing a deep clean of the mansion," was what Wormwood had said. "Wormwood's trying out a new recipe in the kitchen," was what Maribelle had said.)

I would have forbidden it immediately, in case another innocent person gets arrested for no good reason, continued Edie. She peered at each of the guests' faces with her glassy gray eyes before stitching, *I don't believe any of you were at the last party.*

"No, we weren't," Ms. H agreed quickly.

Our whole family was toppled because of the Incident. Edie paused. *What are your names?*

Dewey blinked. Edie didn't seem to remember the Hs at all. So Wormwood must have been lying. Edie obviously *didn't* recognize every face from the party thirteen years ago.... But why had Wormwood been so insistent? It was almost as if the caretaker didn't want them to talk to Edie, for some reason.

The Hs introduced themselves. Edie turned to Dewey next, her gray eyes piercing his.

"I-I'm Dewey," he said.

A lovely family, Edie stitched, looking at the three of them.

"Oh, they're not my parents," Dewey quickly said. "My dad's downstairs."

Where's your mother?

"She left my dad shortly after I was born."

The Hs' vacant faces turned into ones of sympathy. Edie stared at Dewey for several more seconds, a trace of pity in her gray eyes. Dewey felt his face burn and said,

"It's fine. I never really knew her. My dad and I traveled a lot, so we couldn't keep in touch easily." It was hard to miss someone he didn't know. "Do you, um, have time to answer some questions?" he added, changing the subject.

What about?

"We wanted to know what happened at the party thirteen years ago," said Dewey.

Edie's fingers didn't move for a few moments. *I do not like discussing it.*

"If it helps, we also believe Mort's innocent. We think we can help release him and catch the real culprit."

At this, Edie blinked several times. Then she rapidly began embroidering again. The room was silent as the Hs and Dewey read her answer.

It was so long ago. Nothing seemed out of the ordinary that evening, at first. It was a party like many before it. At one point, the mayor's daughter and I were in the game room together. I watched her play chess against a tall, serious gentleman. After she lost, I left to rejoin the party down the hall. Edie's mouth hardened, and her fingers fumbled with the needle. *We were all shocked when she disappeared. But it was the mayor's fault for bringing a child to this house in the first place.*

"Did the person who played chess with Beatrice leave the room at the same time as you?" asked Dewey.

No, he stayed behind. Edie paused, her eyes fixed on something in the distance. *I remember one incident from that night clearly. The mayor had a dispute with one of the guests. They were arguing at the party.*

"Who was he arguing with?"

It was with a woman who always wears a veil over her face. I remember she wore a great big dress, like a candy drop.

"What were they arguing about?" asked Mr. H.

Edie glanced at Mr. H with a startled expression, as if she had forgotten his presence. *I do not know. All I remember is that she stormed off in the middle of the party and didn't return until the very end.*

"Okay." Dewey made a mental note to jot that down later. "And what do you know about the scarecrow?"

Edie's gray eyes glinted. *What scarecrow?*

Ms. H interrupted, "Never mind. We're running out of time. Your spinning wheel... Can you please tell us more about it?"

Dewey's cheeks flushed. He supposed it was easier to check the spinning wheel than to continue asking questions. But he found it hard to believe that Edie had never discovered the scarecrow in her old room. There was definitely something strange going on.

So, you are curious about my oldest possession.

Slowly, the old woman got up. She seated herself on a wheelchair nearby and carefully navigated across the room. The three guests followed.

Edie stopped in front of a large, old sheet covering what looked like a misshapen couch. *This spinning wheel has been with me for ages.*

Mr. H gripped the sheet and uncovered one section, revealing not a lumpy couch but a wooden wheel no bigger than a small bicycle's. Each spoke of the wheel was intricately carved, and the wood was smooth and checkered.

Edie's sewing needle glinted. *I did not say you could touch it.*

Mr. H apologized and quickly placed the sheet back over the wheel. "Have you used this before?" he asked.

Yes, many times, Edie wrote. *I don't use it as much anymore.* The old woman's lips curled into a tiny smile. *This is the hardiest spinning wheel I've ever known. It can spin anything into fabric. Anything at all.*

It sounded like something from one of those tales that Chaucer collected. Ms. H. repeated, "Anything?"

Yes. Cotton. Spiderwebs. Silver. Skin.

A chill ran down Dewey's spine. He tried to remind himself that Edie couldn't harm him, not when he was in the presence of two other witnesses. She was probably just talking about leather anyway, which was made from the hide of various animals. Still, he took several steps backward, bumping into a chaise lounge.

"So . . . um . . ." Dewey racked his brain for something to say. "Why did you move out of your old room?"

Edie's needle twitched. *The previous room had a strange presence. I did not like it.* She paused. *I noticed it the night of the party.*

Dewey thought back to Dr. Foozle's saying a person's essence never disappeared. It must have been from the scarecrow, he realized with another shiver.

Ms. H put a comforting hand on Dewey's shoulder. He jumped before realizing it was the teacher. Dewey found it astonishing how easy it was to overlook the Hs. It was as if they were an optical illusion, fading into their surroundings. It reminded Dewey of something he'd read in a psychology book once called the Troxler effect.

"It's safest if you leave the room," Ms. H said in a

soft voice so that the others couldn't hear. "We can take it from here."

Dewey was torn. He wanted to leave—immediately, if possible—but he also wanted to see the spindle himself. But Ms. H gave him a reassuring squeeze of the shoulder, and Dewey nodded.

"I, um, have to go," he announced to Edie. "My dad's probably wondering where I am."

Edie wrote something on her pillow, but Dewey had already stumbled across the room for the door, knocking his shin against a stool. Out in the empty corridor, panting slightly, he put on his goggles again and turned to his list of suspects. He jotted down a new entry.

Suspect 8: Edie
Mort Amadeus's mother.

After a moment, he added,

Most likely suspect.

Chapter Sixteen

ONE AND A HALF HOURS UNTIL MIDNIGHT

Back in the library, the remaining group members had not noticed that the Hs or Dewey were missing. After debating the best way to talk to Edie, with Wormwood shaking his head at every suggestion, the group returned to the dining hall, and the conversation somehow shifted to the subject of fried fish. ("It's all about the sauce you use," Duchess von Pelt was telling the group. "Now, have I told you about my award-winning recipes . . . ?")

A few feet away, next to the wall, Wormwood refrained from rolling his eyes as the guests chattered. Midnight was quickly approaching, yet the guests seemed almost ready to give up. *Humans and their short attention spans,* he thought scathingly. *Did Mort and Maribelle really think this would work?* Under his top hat, the caretaker's eyes flicked over the six guests. His mind blanked for a moment. He thought there had been more people in the room.

Then one of them dashed into the dining hall, panting. It was the boy with the goggles.

"Where were you?" Wormwood demanded.

"B-bathroom," Dewey mumbled, sitting down beside the wall. His face was pale. "Stomachache."

"You poor thing," Mrs. Raven said. She poured Dewey a cup of tea.

"Just sit it out, it'll go away soon," Chaucer said. To the others he added, "We've had our share of stomachaches from eating dubious foods during our travels."

Dr. Foozle adjusted his spectacles and studied Dewey's face from afar. The pharmacist had years of experience in medicine—he could tell right away that the quiver in Dewey's body was not due to a stomachache. *The boy's frightened about something,* Dr. Foozle noted.

"Yes, stomachaches are a nuisance," said Duchess von Pelt. "Why, I remember one time I had a mild stomachache after my idiot of a cook bought scallions instead of green onions for my soup. . . ."

Those are the same thing, Dewey wanted to say, but Count Baines interrupted the duchess. "You have a personal cook? I thought all those 'award-winning recipes' were your own."

"What a silly question, darling. Every truly wealthy family has a personal cook."

Chaucer pulled out his notebook. "Aha, that reminds me of another story!" Before the others could groan or roll their eyes, Chaucer had begun.

Once upon a time, in the mountains of central Europe, there was a prominent, wealthy family—

"*How* wealthy, exactly?" interrupted Duchess von Pelt.

"I'm getting to that," said Chaucer, and he continued.

They had a great fortune, enough to buy a small country these days. They were so rich that even their hair was made of gold. The family lived in their secluded castle on top of a steep hill that overlooked the mountains and trees on the horizon.

One day, a girl claiming to be a lonely little orphan was found on their doorstep. The family was perplexed. The girl did not seem like a regular orphan, like the famous one who wore rags covered in ashes and spoke to mice. There were no holes in her clothes, nor were they dirty. In fact, her dress rivaled some of the family's nicest outfits. She also spoke with the confidence of a queen.

The girl turned out to be a particularly persuasive child. Within minutes, the family agreed to set up the biggest room in the castle for her and invited her in.

Over the years, the family ran all sorts of errands for the child. One family member reportedly traveled around the world in order to find a specific brand of chocolates that she liked. Another bought out all the homes in the neighboring town because the child wanted giant houses to store her hundreds of dolls.

Then one morning, just before the girl became of age, something strange happened. The family woke up and walked out of the castle, as if in a trance. They left behind all of their money and valuables. All of their belongings, including the deed to the castle, had been left to the girl.

Meanwhile, the family disappeared and was never seen again.

"Oh crows," murmured Mrs. Raven. "That's awful."

"*I* see nothing awful about it," countered Duchess von Pelt, whose cheeks were flushed underneath her veil. "I'm sure the family's perfectly fine wherever they are. Besides, things disappear all the time. Socks, keys, hairpins, children . . ."

Something about Chaucer's story sounded familiar to Judge Ophelius. He pulled on the curls of his wig, deep in thought. *That's right,* the judge suddenly remembered—there *was* a court case many years ago in which a prominent duke and his family claimed they had been under a spell. The family insisted that the unknown person who had done it had stolen their entire fortune, including their name, which they had lost all memory of.

Judge Ophelius furrowed his eyebrows. "Where do you collect these stories of yours, Chaucer?"

The traveling story collector smiled mysteriously. "Anywhere and everywhere. The information is all out there. The fun part is piecing them together. An anecdote here, a rumor there... They're all part of the same spiderweb, stories connected to one another by fine threads."

While the others talked, Dewey inched next to Wormwood. "Sorry, I have a question," he said quietly.

"Mm-hmm?" the caretaker responded.

"When Edie moved to the attic, how come she left behind a bunch of things in her old room? Wouldn't she have taken those with her?"

Smart kid, Wormwood thought. *Maybe he'll solve this thing before anyone else does.* "She requested we leave her old furniture behind," he answered. "Said they contained an aura of bad luck."

Dewey looked at the caretaker questioningly, and Wormwood shrugged one shoulder.

"Edie's very old, so we don't . . . question her about these things," Wormwood explained. "The only item from her room that she took up with her was her prized spinning wheel."

Dewey nodded and scribbled something in his book. "Thank you. This is useful."

"Excuse us, we have an important announcement." Two people appeared at the doorway. It took the guests a few moments to remember their names.

"We've spoken to Edie," Mr. H told everyone. Ms. H stood next to him. Their expressions were difficult to read. The specter hound scurried to the schoolteacher and tried to paw at her hands, its ears perked.

"You talked to Edie?" Wormwood said, stunned.

"Yes, we visited her in the attic while you guys were debating over what to do," said Ms. H. "She was very welcoming. I believe she's actually missed having visitors."

Dr. Foozle turned to face Wormwood and said pointedly, "But didn't you tell us earlier that Edie refused to speak with any of us?"

The caretaker didn't answer. He simply gaped in the Hs' direction, amazed—or perhaps frightened.

"Edie does own a spinning wheel," continued Mr. H. "We've confirmed it. We wanted to see whether it was cursed. . . ."

Ms. H held something in her cupped hands. "We've decided to bring you the evidence ourselves," she said.

She held out her hands for the group to see. In her palms was a wooden spindle, the tip dark red and luminous as a flame.

The spindle was slowly passed around the group. Most of the guests were puzzled about what they were looking at, but when Judge Ophelius examined it between his fingers, he let out a sharp exhale. "It's cursed, all right," the judge confirmed. He squinted at the schoolteacher. "You obtained the spindle from Edie's spinning wheel?"

"Yes, we took it when she had her back turned," said Ms. H. "She didn't notice because she keeps the spinning wheel covered all the time."

The others faced Judge Ophelius with worried expressions. "What does this all mean, Judge?" Dr. Foozle asked.

Judge Ophelius gripped his walking cane and stood.

"It means," he said in a low voice, "that we may have arrested the wrong member of the Amadeus family."

The dining hall suddenly felt colder than before.

"Well, what are we waiting for?" exclaimed Duchess von Pelt, breaking the silence. "We have less than two hours until the case closes forever. Let's have Edie arrested immediately!"

"Hang on a minute," interrupted Chaucer. "All we know is the enchanted spindle thingy was found on Edie's spinning wheel. It doesn't mean *she* was the one who turned Beatrice Willoughby into the scarecrow."

"The scarecrow was found in her old room, darling," the duchess shot back. "I'm not sure how much more proof you need."

Chaucer shook his head. "But it doesn't mean she's guilty! Any one of us could have lured Beatrice Willoughby upstairs that night."

This simpleton's going to get us all arrested if he doesn't shut up, thought Count Baines. "I'm in favor of arresting Edie," he said aloud. He added to Chaucer, "Be careful not to spill your tea in thirty seconds."

Chaucer moved aside the teacup in front of him. "I'm just saying it doesn't add up," he insisted. "I remember Edie being a really sweet person. There can't be a crime without a…what's the word? *Motive.* The criminal always has a reason. But Edie has no reason for kidnapping children and enchanting them!"

Dewey quietly disagreed. As discussed earlier, children's hearts increased one's lifespan, and there was no doubt Edie had been living a longer-than-average life.

"The spindle is proof, isn't it?" Mrs. Raven gulped down another cup of tea. "Oh crows…just when you think you know a person…"

Tap-tap-tap. Judge Ophelius brought the room to order with his walking cane.

"Now would be a good time for the host to explain himself," the judge said to Wormwood.

Wormwood had remained still as a statue beside the wall. Now, he fidgeted woodenly under Judge Ophelius's intense gaze. "You don't—you don't actually *believe* all this, Your Honor?" he sputtered.

"Then how do you explain the spindle?"

"I have no idea." Wormwood pointed wildly at the Hs. "They must have planted it as fake evidence!"

Duchess von Pelt let out a derisive laugh. Several other guests also gave Wormwood a dubious look. "Ah, perhaps you were protecting Edie all along," Dr. Foozle said, wiping his spectacles with his coat. "Why didn't I see it before? You were hoping to free Mort from prison by falsely pinning the crime on one of us, weren't you?"

"Nonsense," Wormwood argued. "They just—impossible—obviously a setup!" Unfortunately, the more the caretaker tried to defend Edie, the guiltier he sounded.

Duchess von Pelt wore a triumphant smirk. "That's exactly what happened, Doctor. They clearly invited us here in the hopes that one of us would take the fall for Edie's crime!" she said. "Or *crimes,* should I say? I wouldn't be surprised if she's responsible for all those missing kids over the years, stealing their hearts!"

She sure seems confident that Edie is guilty, Dewey noticed. More than confident, in fact—the duchess seemed almost determined that Edie was the culprit.

Judge Ophelius stood up straight. "In light of the new evidence uncovered tonight, I have no choice but to place Edie Amadeus under arrest." He cast his gaze on Wormwood. "Unless you have something new to add?"

It was not Wormwood but Chaucer who jumped up to block the judge's path.

"Please, Judge, you're making a big mistake," he pleaded. "Edie is innocent. All of the Amadeuses are innocent. I'm sure of it!"

He certainly seems confident that Edie is not *guilty,* thought Judge Ophelius.

Mrs. Raven went up to Chaucer and placed a comforting hand on his shoulder. "I understand you aren't from around here," she said gently. "Over the past thirteen years, many of the townspeople have had doubts about the Amadeus family. Beatrice Willoughby's disappearance shook us all."

"Then why did you come to the party tonight, given your suspicions?" challenged Chaucer.

"W-well, nobody knows the truth," admitted Mrs. Raven, clearing her throat. "We had *suspicions,* that's all . . . and their parties have always been enjoyable. . . ."

"Exactly." Chaucer crossed his arms. "The Amadeuses could very well be innocent."

Duchess von Pelt was less gracious than the innkeeper; her patience was at its limit. "Stop wasting time," she snapped. "Summon the police so they can arrest Edie and get this over with!"

"Huh, interesting," spoke up Count Baines. The others turned to look at the count, who was reading his pocket watch with a mildly amused look. "Guess the hosts were telling the truth after all," he added.

"I beg your pardon?" asked Judge Ophelius.

"Nothing." Count Baines put away his pocket watch. "I just saw the future."

There was a tense silence.

"What did you see?" Mrs. Raven finally asked.

Count Baines's voice returned to his usual bored tone. He shrugged. "One of the guests gets arrested before midnight. It isn't Edie."

Several people's jaws dropped. "It's... not?" said Ms. H.

Count Baines shook his head.

"Who is it, then?" demanded Judge Ophelius impatiently.

Count Baines shrugged again. "The duchess."

Chapter Seventeen

ONE HOUR AND FIFTEEN MINUTES UNTIL MIDNIGHT

The duchess's lips twisted into an amused smile as she looked at the alarmed faces around her. "You have got to be kidding me," she said. "Didn't we just agree that Edie is the one who owns a spinning wheel? Not to mention the scarecrow was found in *her room*."

"But...but why else would *you* get arrested later?" said Mrs. Raven, clutching her chest. The crow on her shoulder squawked.

The others pestered Count Baines for an explanation. Count Baines gave an annoyed sigh. *Simpletons, the lot of them.* He leaned back in his chair and said impatiently, "All I saw was the duchess getting handcuffed by the police in exactly"—the count took out his pocket watch—"twenty minutes."

"How accurate are your predictions?" Judge Ophelius asked.

"They're always accurate," the count answered.

"So then Duchess von Pelt must be the culprit responsible," said Ms. H, sounding bewildered.

"Hang on," said Dewey. "He only *predicted* the duchess gets arrested. If we end up naming her as the culprit, then it's only because of Count Baines's prediction. It's not because we have real evidence pinning her." He looked around the room, waiting for the others' reaction. "Don't you see? It's not logical."

"Ah, but we do have evidence," pointed out Dr. Foozle. "Remember Beatrice's drawings from the study? One of them had the face scribbled out, hiding the person's features like a veil."

Judge Ophelius took out the notepad from his cloak and turned to the page in question. His gaze went from the picture to the duchess and back again. "Yes, that's right, Doctor," he murmured.

"Come to think of it..." Mr. H stepped forward, his muddy eyes fixed on the duchess. "Edie mentioned the mayor had gotten into a big argument with one of the party guests on the same night Beatrice Willoughby disappeared. From the descriptions, there was no doubt Edie was describing Duchess von Pelt."

"Oh crows, yes, I remember the argument between them," said Mrs. Raven. Next to her, Chaucer nodded.

The atmosphere in the room shifted. Count Baines's prediction had redirected the others' suspicions, placing the duchess at the center of the spotlight. Suddenly, everything they had learned before seemed to prove the duchess's guilt. *Not the duchess, it can't be....* Duchess von Pelt, with all her flowers and pretty gloves, a kidnapper, a killer? It seemed hard to believe. Yet, she certainly seemed like the kind of person who took things personally.... Maybe she had enchanted Beatrice as revenge against Mayor Willoughby....

"You're all being ridiculous," said the duchess, her voice hard. "Don't look at me like that. You think I—*I*,

Duchess von Pelt of the von Pelt family—bewitched Beatrice and ate her heart?"

"But your real name is not von Pelt, is it?" said Judge Ophelius in a low voice.

Duchess von Pelt gaped at the judge like he had just slapped her across the face. "Ex-excuse me?"

"The story from earlier... that girl who tricked the family into giving up their wealth... That was you, wasn't it?"

"How can you say—now, *really*—that's ridiculous—"

"You hypnotized Duke von Pelt and his family, then stole everything they had," Judge Ophelius said calmly over the duchess's outrage. "It was many cases ago, but Chaucer's story triggered the memory."

"Stories do have that effect," agreed Chaucer, his eyes twinkling.

Duchess von Pelt poured herself a cup of tea, her gloved hands shaking. After a long moment, she said quietly, "Well done. You're the first one ever to figure out my past."

Gasps filled the dining hall.

The duchess looked around the room. When

she spoke again, there was a trace of bitterness in her voice.

"I was born unwanted," the duchess said. "My real parents left me in a cabinet inside an abandoned apartment. When the orphanage staff found me, they told me my last name was Caligari, but I didn't have a first name. I was penniless and alone. I had nobody. But as I grew older, I realized I was particularly . . . persuasive. I learned how to make people adore me."

She paused to sip her tea. A few of the guests eyed each other. None of them knew where this was headed.

"I grew up envious of the children who came from wealthy families," Duchess von Pelt continued. "Even though I had a lot of talents, I had nothing to my name. Meanwhile, these other children—some of whom were the most boring, dull kids imaginable—got everything they wanted. It was dreadfully unfair. So I decided to do something about it. Over the years, I convinced multiple families to adopt me. All of them were wealthy, well-respected folks. I learned their ways before moving on to the next family."

It felt good to finally reveal her past, as though a weight had been lifted off her shoulders. She stood and drew herself up to her full height. Her eyes swept over the room. Good, everyone's eyes were on her, even the two guests in the back—what were their names again? Whatever, it didn't matter. The duchess adjusted her veil.

"Little by little, I amassed a grand fortune," she said. "I don't consider what I did stealing, so much as *borrowing*. The only people I really stole from were bumbling jerks. Like Mayor Willoughby. He's a pompous and power-hungry fool. At the Amadeuses' last party, we indeed got into a heated argument. I can tell you what we argued about. He insisted that salad forks should be room temperature. Yes, it's absurd. All salad forks should be chilled—a good salad should be cold and crisp, and so should the utensil that delivers it. I learned this from one of the families I stayed with."

Judge Ophelius rapped his walking cane. "But stealing is still stealing," he said to the duchess. "You admit you were a thief, then?"

"Sure, I admit it," Duchess von Pelt said easily. "But only because none of you will remember this moment afterward."

She stood tall and removed her veil, her face in full

view. The others blinked at her. As they made eye contact with the duchess, an odd expression passed over their faces, one by one.

"There we go," the duchess said, watching their impassive faces with a smile. "Now, darlings, why don't we start with an apology to yours truly?"

The people in the dining hall spoke in unison, their syllables in perfect harmony: "We are sorry, Duchess."

"Sorry for what?" Duchess von Pelt sang. "Be *specific.*"

"We are sorry we accused you."

One person did not speak. Near the back of the room, Dewey looked around, bewildered at everyone's sudden change of heart. He took off his goggles and looked closer at the duchess's face—he had thought her eyes looked a bit weird and was wondering if his goggles were distorting his vision. But he was shocked to realize he had been right: the duchess's eyes were not normal but were large and bright red, the same shade as his goggles when they lit up. They seemed to swirl like whirlpools, tugging the viewer in.

Duchess von Pelt was not looking in Dewey's direction. "Now then," she said with a flourish. "Let's get to the bottom of this mystery once and for all. I am quite certain Edie's the true culprit, but while I have you here... there are some questions I have for each of you. Some... *secrets* you might be hiding that I'd like revealed."

The others waited obediently. Duchess von Pelt started on the right side of the table. She pointed a gloved finger at Dr. Foozle. "I bet some of your concoctions in your pharmacy are downright illegal, Doctor. Isn't that right?"

Dr. Foozle twitched under the duchess's fiery red eyes. His words seemed to be wrenched out of him against his will. "Y-yes, that's ri—that's right."

"Do you keep a record of such sales in your store?" asked Duchess von Pelt.

"I keep a—a ledger, yes."

The duchess held out her hand expectantly. Dr. Foozle reluctantly reached into the inside of his lab coat and took out a bulky book with black leather binding. Duchess von Pelt grabbed the ledger and went through the pages.

"Interesting," she said, reading the ledger. "Wormwood apparently paid you handsomely for a vial of bone dust earlier."

Wormwood acknowledged Duchess von Pelt's remark with a simple dip of his head.

"But you're not responsible for turning Beatrice Willoughby into a scarecrow, are you?" the duchess said to Dr. Foozle.

"No, I had nothing to do with that," Dr. Foozle replied. "I no longer engage in that sort of dark magic, ever since my grandfather's great-granduncle's big experiment with reanimated corpses went awry."

Duchess von Pelt seemed satisfied. "And what about you?" she said to Mrs. Raven. "There's something unusual going on at that inn of yours with all those birds."

"Oh crows, I'm very fond of the creatures," Mrs. Raven murmured. "I've liked them ever since I was a child. A crow helped me spy on my rival's birthday party that I wasn't invited to.... The crow relayed to me everything they said behind my back. Since then I've depended on crows as my eyes and ears."

"I see." Duchess von Pelt looked skeptically at the crow perched on Mrs. Raven's shoulder. "So that crow you have there, I'm guessing you two are familiar with each other?"

Mrs. Raven blushed. "I... I was the one who brought

him to the party thirteen years ago... hidden inside a pie. After Beatrice disappeared, investigators swarmed the place. I couldn't leave with the crow in tow, so I left him here."

Only Dewey gasped at this startling news. The others continued to sit woodenly in their seats, their eyes glued to the duchess.

They've been hypnotized! Dewey finally realized. Duchess von Pelt's red eyes had hypnotic powers... but why wasn't the hypnosis affecting him? Even as the question formed in his mind, the answer occurred to Dewey: *the goggles.* His copper goggles must be blocking the duchess's powers the way sunglasses blocked harmful rays from the sun. He quickly put them back on again.

Duchess von Pelt turned to the count next. "Seeing into the future sure is handy, Count Baines," she said. "I wonder if you've ever used it for a... *dishonest* reason?"

Count Baines clenched his fingers around his pocket watch. For a moment, it seemed like he was going to remain silent. But under the duchess's intense gaze, his mouth struggled from side to side, like something was fighting its way out. Finally, he said unwillingly, "It—it helps when you're playing games."

"Games?" repeated Duchess von Pelt with a smirk. "So you cheat in games regularly? What kinds of games?"

"Card games . . . chess . . . checkers . . . Any kind of game is easy when you can see the next moves."

"Chess, hmm?" The duchess crossed her arms. "Wasn't Beatrice Willoughby playing chess with someone at the party thirteen years ago?"

Count Baines gave a curt nod. "That was me. I won all three games."

The duchess let out an airy laugh. "You're kidding me. You, a grown *adult,* cheated in a chess game against a six-year-old?"

"She was quite clever for her age, actually. Much better than her father."

While Duchess von Pelt interrogated Count Baines, Dewey inched toward the table where his dad was sitting. "Dad, are you okay?" he whispered.

Chaucer blinked a few times at Dewey before beaming. "Never better, son! Now we know the duchess is no longer a suspect."

"But—" Dewey said. He stopped speaking and shrank back when the duchess's eyes flicked toward them.

"What about you?" Duchess von Pelt now faced Chaucer and Dewey, her red eyes unblinking.

Pretend you're hypnotized. "W-we're travelers," Dewey said in a higher-than-usual voice. "We can't be the suspects, because we weren't even invited to tonight's party."

Chaucer shook his head. "Actually, the hosts asked me to come," he said cheerfully. "Got a special invitation in the mail. I was invited for a very special reason."

Dewey stared at his dad. Was the duchess playing with his dad's memory? "No, we weren't," Dewey reminded him. "Wormwood had to ask the hosts if we could stay, remember?"

"No, no, it was all part of the plan," Chaucer reassured Dewey. "It was meant to be a secret. I daresay only Mort and Maribelle knew about it."

Now we're getting somewhere, Duchess von Pelt thought. It was too bad none of the people in the room would remember this moment—she was almost as fantastic a detective as she was at everything else. "And why did they invite you?" she said, studying Chaucer's face. "Are you an undercover reporter? Or perhaps"—her eyes flashed—"you were involved in the plot to steal Beatrice Willoughby's heart!"

Dewey's own heart hammered in his chest. He thought back to what Wormwood had emphasized multiple times: *the hosts had invited each of them that night for a reason*. Maybe his dad really had been invited, but it was obviously meant to be a secret from the others—including his own son. Dewey had to distract them before his dad said something incriminating.

He picked up one of the teacups. In one sudden movement, he flung the cup across the floor. It shattered, sending porcelain shards and hot liquid everywhere.

The noise made everyone in the room jump, breaking their attention away from Duchess von Pelt. It also seemed to break the spell.

"Dewey!" scolded Chaucer, shaking his head at the mess.

"It's all right," said Wormwood with an impatient sigh. "I will get the mop."

The duchess blocked the caretaker's path before he could leave. "Oh, no you won't," she said. "I've been curious about *your* role in this whole conspiracy."

Wormwood's body stiffened. "What do you mean?"

"Do you expect us to trust you, when you won't even show us your face?"

The other guests found that strange coming from the duchess, who had kept her own face hidden most of the night, but they kept their mouths shut.

Duchess von Pelt adjusted her veil and fixed her gaze on the caretaker. "What exactly are you hiding underneath that hat and scarf of yours, darling?"

Abruptly, Wormwood seemed to be bound in place, as if tied by invisible ropes. He struggled and fell to the ground, immobile. Then, to everyone's enormous surprise, the caretaker began to float. The specter hound jumped and ran in circles underneath the hovering body, yapping noiselessly. Several guests shrieked.

Wormwood, it turned out, had no feet—nor legs or arms. Instead, wooden stilts and metal hooks clattered to the floor below. The jacket collapsed to the floor in a shriveled pile, strings hanging from the inside. Wormwood's top hat rolled off his head, and his scarf unraveled from around his face. What remained was a furry gray bat.

Chapter Eighteen

ONE HOUR UNTIL MIDNIGHT

"Fine, you've caught me," Wormwood said, flapping open his wings and facing the stunned guests. "It was rather cumbersome moving around in that thing anyway."

The discovery that the Amadeuses' caretaker was a bat spooked the guests more than anything else had that night. The grandfather clock chimed eleven, but the group hardly noticed. Duchess von Pelt swooned and sat down, her veil flopping back over her face. Mrs. Raven poured herself a ninth cup of tea, trembling. Judge Ophelius leaned against his walking cane for support. Even Count Baines wore a startled expression on his face.

"Oh, come on," said Wormwood, frowning at the others' reactions—if bats could frown. "Let's not all jump and hug at the same time now, shall we? Yes, I am a bat. *Not* a vampire bat, by the way. I find human blood tastes rather disgusting."

"How can you talk?" breathed Duchess von Pelt.

Dr. Foozle adjusted his spectacles with a shaky hand. "Ah, he must have drunk several drops of Essence of Babel, a special elixir that gives animals the ability to communicate with humans. Extremely complicated to brew, and costs more than a house. Only a handful of animals throughout history have been able to drink some, usually the pets of kings or rich noblemen. I believe I sold one...let me see..." He patted his lab coat for several moments before noticing his ledger on the table, out in the open. "How'd this get here?"

The others shrugged.

Dr. Foozle picked the black book up, making sure to keep its pages away from the others' prying eyes, and started going through the pages one by one. "I'm fairly certain Maribelle Amadeus bought a bottle from my pharmacy years and years ago.... Let's see now..."

"Searching the whole thing is going to take an hour and fifty-nine minutes," said Count Baines. "To save us time, the entry in question is on page 112."

"Ah, thank you, Count Baines." Dr. Foozle ran his finger down a list of sales made twelve years ago. "Yes, here it is. '*One bottle of Essence of Babel, sold to Maribelle Amadeus.*' Cost a fortune, those things."

"Yes, the Amadeuses needed a way to understand me after I was hired as their caretaker," Wormwood said matter-of-factly.

"They *hired* you?" said Ms. H.

"They find that bats are more reliable than humans. We move a lot quicker, when we're not being stifled by these clunky human clothes. I can fly to places undetected and move from house to house in a blink." Wormwood's beady black eyes fixed on Judge Ophelius. "That was how I was able to drop off the note on your doorstep earlier and disappear before you came out."

Judge Ophelius reached into his pocket and took out a crumpled piece of paper. He read the note aloud for the others, *"In case you're having second thoughts about tonight, Your Honor, don't."* He raised an eyebrow at Wormwood. "*You* sent me this?"

"The hosts asked me to," the bat answered. "They wanted to make sure you of all people didn't back out at the last minute."

Of course. Only Judge Ophelius had the power to sentence the real culprit to prison on the spot.

"Why did you disguise yourself as a human?" asked Chaucer.

"Why?" Wormwood scoffed and gestured to the group. "Because of reactions like this, that's why."

"I think a talking bat is . . . marvelous," said Mrs. Raven unconvincingly. She wondered if Wormwood had ever spied on her in town without her knowing. The thought gave her an uneasy feeling. Spying and eavesdropping was only fine when *she* did it.

While the others' attention was focused on Wormwood, Dewey approached his dad again. Under his breath, he asked, "What did you mean when you said the Amadeuses gave you an invitation?"

"What?" Chaucer paused with his pumpkin chip in midair and eyed Dewey with raised eyebrows. "I never said they invited me."

Dewey frowned. "But earlier, you told Duchess von Pelt—"

"No, no, son. I wouldn't even be here if Mrs. Raven hadn't convinced the caretaker to let us in."

Mrs. Raven, who overheard their conversation, said ruefully, "I'm sorry I dragged you into this."

"Don't be sorry! It was a great decision." Chaucer gave the innkeeper a thumbs-up. "Very...what's the word? *Eventful.*"

Dewey didn't say anything. Was he the only one who had any recollection of what had happened in the last ten minutes? It appeared so. One thing was certain: his dad knew more than he was letting on.

"Right then, where were we?" said Duchess von Pelt, straightening. "It's clear the Amadeuses have been tricking us from the beginning." She turned to face Chaucer. "And it appears *one* of the guests is in on the whole thing—!"

The doorbell suddenly rang.

The guests stopped talking. Wormwood sounded

perplexed. "That's unexpected," he murmured. "I don't remember inviting any more guests. . . ."

He tried to wriggle back inside his jacket. The doorbell rang again, an urgent chime. Wormwood struggled with the sleeves before giving up.

He looked at Judge Ophelius. "Er, do you mind answering the door with me, Your Honor? I'm afraid most people don't take kindly to talking bats."

Not in the mood for any more surprises that night, Judge Ophelius reluctantly nodded. He and Wormwood left the room.

The rest of the group was perturbed. "Who could it be at this late an hour?" asked Mrs. Raven.

"A late guest, perhaps," guessed Dr. Foozle.

"And Wormwood got mad at me for coming *early*," scoffed Duchess von Pelt.

A moment later, Wormwood and Judge Ophelius returned to the dining hall. They were accompanied by the town florist and a policeman.

"There she is!" the florist said, pointing dramatically at Duchess von Pelt. "We've caught her at last, the flower thief. Look, she's sewn my tulips onto her dress!"

Duchess von Pelt's face turned crimson under her veil. The others were too baffled to say anything.

The policeman swung a pair of handcuffs from his wrist and explained to the judge, "She's been stealing flowers from all over town. We saw her steal some from a windowsill just before she disappeared into the Inkwoods." He added it had taken them a while to find the house. "Turns out you can get as lost as a sunken ship in these woods," he commented.

The guests gaped at the newcomers. "But then—the prediction—" They turned to look at Count Baines.

"Told you," the count yawned.

"You didn't mention it was for *stealing flowers,*" said Judge Ophelius testily.

Duchess von Pelt was annoyed. She reached for her veil. Time for another little hypnosis... No, it didn't matter. She could handle a simple charge like a flower theft easily—she'd gotten out of it many times before. Anyway, it was about time she left this dreadful party.

"Fine, fine, let's get this over with," she said, holding out her arms. "Mind the sleeves, please. The tulip petals are delicate."

As the policeman clicked the handcuffs around

her wrists and led her away, she faced the group with a smile and gave a small curtsy, as if she were a performer exiting the stage. "Don't worry about me, darlings," she called out. "You have bigger problems tonight. Figure out who's responsible for poor Beatrice Willoughby, why don't you?"

After the duchess and the newcomers left, the group members digested the information that Duchess von Pelt had been a trifling flower thief. Mrs. Raven and the crow quickly put their heads together and began gossiping about all they now suspected of the duchess—how she probably picked the types of flowers to steal depending on the weather, and how she'd once worn a coat stitched with forty white roses to the Yuletide Parade that likely had come from a neighbor's garden...

Several guests asked Judge Ophelius how long a jail sentence Duchess von Pelt would get.

"Considering her spotless record, none," the judge replied. He added with a hint of disapproval, "Plus, as she comes from a famous and influential family, I am certain she would be able to secure excellent lawyers."

"What did she mean when she said one of the guests

is in on the whole thing?" Mrs. Raven wondered out loud. "I feel I might've missed something."

"The duchess was looking at Chaucer when she said it," said Dr. Foozle, who also felt like he had missed some important clue but refused to admit it.

"She hypnotized you all," spoke up Dewey, ready to defend his dad. He was unsure of his dad's role, but whatever it was, he had to make sure the others did not find out the truth. It could be important for catching the real culprit.

"What do you mean *hypnotized?*" snapped Mr. H.

"A while ago, before the police and the florist came," explained Dewey. "She asked a bunch of questions and then wiped your memories."

"*What?*" exclaimed several guests.

"Her real name is something Caligari, and she was left in a cabinet as a child. She asked each of you to explain your past."

There was a pause. The others glanced at one another. Was the boy telling the truth? If so, what secrets had each of them unwittingly revealed?

"I don't recall any of this," said Count Baines.

"Me neither," said Mrs. Raven quickly.

Dewey sighed impatiently. "That's because you were *under a trance*."

"And *you* weren't?"

"Well, no. I think my goggles had something to do with it. They're meant to protect the eyes."

Wormwood tilted his furry head. "Makes sense," he said. "What kind of questions did the duchess ask?"

"That's quite enough," spoke up Ms. H. She gave Judge Ophelius a concerned look. "Aren't we forgetting Wormwood could be in on this whole thing?"

"*Please!*" the caretaker sighed, exasperated. "Do you really think I wanted to reveal my true form, lady?"

A few guests began debating whether the duchess was the culprit after all. Amid the commotion, Dewey quietly slipped away unnoticed. The others were going in circles, and he needed space to think. He knew the duchess was not responsible for Beatrice Willoughby. Otherwise, she could have easily pinned the blame on one of them using her powers. She had wanted to solve this case as much as he did.

Out in the hallway, Dewey leaned against the wall and reviewed the notes he had gathered so far that evening. Someone had stolen Beatrice's heart, then enchanted her into a scarecrow. Judge Ophelius had mentioned earlier that such magic preserved the body. Could Beatrice's heart be preserved somewhere? Namely, could that spark, the one that kept a person alive, still be around?

There was a more pressing question: Who was the culprit? Dewey closed his eyes. *Think,* he told himself. They didn't have much time left. *Think.* Who?

A cold draft passed by his legs. He glanced down in surprise to see the specter hound at his side, wagging its tail.

"Oh, hi there," Dewey said, bending down to pet the hound. All his hands felt was air, but there was unmistakably a chilly breeze where the specter hound's body was. It licked Dewey with its ghostlike tongue, tickling Dewey's palm.

"Dr. Foozle sure is smart, isn't he?" remarked Dewey. "If it weren't for him, we never would have tracked down the scarecrow. I don't think he is the culprit, despite his knowledge about children's hearts and potions."

The specter hound barked noiselessly. Dewey took it as a sign the creature agreed.

"I don't think Edie's the culprit either, now that I

think about it. She wouldn't have let her son go to jail for something she did." Dewey might not have known his own mother, but he had read about how other moms were—that most of them would do anything for their kids. Yes, there was a chance Edie was innocent, despite the evidence against her. As his dad had said, someone else could have easily used the spinning wheel.

Think, think! He went through the facts. All he knew was that each of the guests had been invited that night for a reason. Including, apparently, his dad. Judge Ophelius was there to acquit Mort, so he couldn't be the culprit. That left Mrs. Raven . . . and Count Baines.

Where would a good detective start? The scene of the crime.

An idea jumped into Dewey's head. He stood up.

"Come on," he said urgently to the specter hound. "I need your help."

Chapter Nineteen

FORTY MINUTES UNTIL MIDNIGHT

Edie sat alone. The attic was silent save for the soft creaking of her rocking chair and the faint chime of the grandfather clock two floors below.

Such was the size of the house that Edie was often left out of the loop on what was happening. She didn't mind. It wasn't as if anything interesting ever happened since her beloved son, Mort, got taken away. She much preferred passing the days away in her quiet corner of the mansion, brooding on the injustice. If only the real culprit confessed. . . .

She knew Maribelle was just as upset about the Incident. Edie would glimpse a fierce gleam in Maribelle's eyes from time to time, and she had long suspected the puppet master of plotting something big.

Edie was unsurprised, therefore, when the two adults and the boy with the weird goggles had appeared in her doorway. She scrunched up her face. What did the two adults look like again? She couldn't remember for the life of her, despite her usually crystal-clear memory.

Edie heard footsteps approaching her door again. Unlike the slow, unsure footsteps earlier that evening, this time the pace of the footfalls was rapid and urgent. Her fingers tightened around the embroidery at her lap.

The door swung open. A shimmering doglike creature sprinted into the room with the boy from earlier.

Edie raised an eyebrow, waiting for an explanation, but Dewey ignored her. He looked around the place distractedly, then walked to the opposite side of the room.

Where are you going? Edie stitched. She shook her pillow in the air for his attention, but Dewey kept walking.

Then Edie realized: the boy was headed for her spinning wheel.

She quickly seated herself onto her wheelchair. "Stop," she tried to call out, but her voice was hoarse from years of disuse.

Dewey had already yanked the cover off her precious spinning wheel by the time Edie rolled across the room. She snatched the sheet from Dewey and then sewed furiously, *What do you think you're doing?!*

"The spindle's missing," Dewey pointed out.

Edie glanced at the spinning wheel, startled. Indeed, the spiky tool was gone.

Someone had taken her spindle. Wormwood? Maribelle? No, those two never went near the spinning wheel. The only people who had seen it in the last decade were the boy and those two adults from earlier. . . . Edie's head snapped up. Her eyes narrowed.

How did you know it was missing? Why are you here?

Dewey took several steps back, keeping a safe distance between himself and Edie. "Do you always keep the spindle there?" he asked.

Of course I do. It is an essential part of the spinning

wheel. Without it, you cannot twist and spin the thread. Now answer my question.

Dewey, meanwhile, was thinking fast. The cursed spindle the Hs had shown everyone earlier indeed seemed to come directly from Edie's spinning wheel, which was now missing a piece. But did he know that for *sure?* Especially since, as several individuals had mentioned, someone could be trying to frame Edie. Someone could have easily swapped the real spindle for the cursed one when Edie hadn't been looking.

He ignored Edie's question and darted for the small bed in the corner. To Edie's surprise, the boy picked up her sleeping pillow.

Insolent child, stop touching my stuff! Did you take my spindle, too? Edie wheeled after the boy, but maneuvering between all the furniture was difficult.

Meanwhile, Dewey plucked something invisible from the pillow. He hurried next to the ghostly doglike creature and held it under its nose. The creature sniffed it, whatever it was, then yelped silently.

While Edie snatched the pillow back from Dewey, the ghostlike hound sniffed the area. It paused in front of Edie and tried to jump on her lap, startling the old woman. She tried to push the animal away, her hands merely touching cold air. Sensing it was unwanted, the creature circled the furniture in the room until it stopped in front of the spinning wheel.

"Very good," Dewey said encouragingly to the hound. "Anywhere else?"

The creature barked again, then doubled back on itself. It sped out the door.

"I'll be back!" Dewey called to Edie before disappearing. The door slammed shut behind them, leaving the woman dazed and bewildered. She reminded herself to ask Wormwood to install a lock on the attic door.

Out in the corridor, Dewey pocketed the strand of white hair he had taken from Edie's pillow. He followed the specter hound down the stairs, his heart thumping with excitement. It wasn't the fun kind of excitement, the kind you might get when you see the book you've been wanting to read is finally available at the bookstore or library. It was the sweaty-palms, stomach-churning, dangerously-close-to-throwing-up kind of excitement, the kind you get while running through a strange, dark mansion to solve a thirteen-year-old mystery before the clock ticks down.

He hoped his plan would work. They went down the second-story corridor, darting past shadows and flickering candles.

The specter hound stopped abruptly. It let out several silent barks.

They were standing in front of Mort's study again.

"We've already been here," Dewey said, feeling disappointed.

The specter hound continued to make barking motions. Dewey pushed the door. It slid open. The specter hound ran across the dark room to the writing desk again. It stood on its hind legs and pawed at the desk drawer.

Using the light from his goggles, Dewey made his way across the room. Through the red light, the hundreds of puppets appeared more ominous than before. They sat staring at him silently from the shelves. His eyes flicked to the one that reminded him of his dad, then did a double take. A shelf below was a puppet of the innkeeper, hunched in a shawl with a tiny black bird on its shoulder.

The specter hound kept yapping for Dewey's attention, but Dewey ignored it. He rapidly scanned the puppets one by one.

All over the shelves, certain puppets began to pop out. You might have experienced something similar, such as when you've bought a new pair of shoes or learned a new word in the dictionary. All of a sudden, you start noticing other people wearing those same shoes or the new word being used everywhere you go. Two puppets now stood out to Dewey, one with its mouth painted in a frown and a pocket watch in its hand, another dressed in a large pink dress and matching veiled hat.

Something cold touched Dewey's legs. The specter hound was now nibbling at him for his attention.

"What is it?" Dewey followed the creature to the desk drawer. The specter hound raised its head expectantly. Dewey carefully opened the drawer.

His stomach lurched. Inside the drawer was a plain wooden spindle with a checkered pattern, the same as Edie's spinning wheel.

"This was not here before," he whispered. The specter hound wagged its tail in confirmation.

Someone had hidden the spindle there after they'd

visited Mort's study. It was a clever move. Nobody would check a room they had already been to.

"Those two guests earlier . . . they showed everyone a different spindle," Dewey said, thinking out loud. "That one had glowed red. They said it belonged to Edie. And now we found another one here." He held up the checkered spindle—with its unique pattern, it clearly belonged to Edie's spinning wheel upstairs, the way a pair of matching shoes belonged together. "Then . . . does that mean Edie has two spindles, one normal and one cursed? But if *that's* true, why would someone hide the normal one? This must be the *real* spindle then, and that means . . ."

"So, you really are a clever boy," said a voice behind him.

Mr. and Ms. H were standing by the door, watching Dewey.

Chapter Twenty

HALF AN HOUR UNTIL MIDNIGHT

The Hs stood still, the light from the hallway casting long shadows over their silhouettes. The specter hound, detecting animosity, bent low into a growling position. Dewey closed his fingers around the spindle and hid it behind his back.

"You passed us a few times," Mr. H said casually. "Didn't notice us once. Made it easy for us to tail you."

"We never understood why some people crave

attention, like the duchess," added Ms. H. "It's much nicer being overlooked. You can get away with *many* things."

Dewey flicked on the reading lamp beside him. Light flooded the room, but it only made the Hs seem more menacing as their plain faces came into view. They peered at him, waiting.

Dewey tried to keep his voice calm. "The cursed spindle was yours, wasn't it? You hid the real spindle and tried to frame Edie."

"Yes, it was extremely amusing," said Ms. H. "Almost as amusing as when we planted that lock of Beatrice's hair next to the chess set at the last party."

The specter hound raised its head and barked noiselessly. The Hs gave a tiny smile. "That rotten creature almost gave us away earlier," Mr. H mentioned. "Kept sniffing my shoe where we store our spindle..." Balancing expertly on one leg, Mr. H swiftly touched the bottom of his heel and took out the shiny scarlet spindle.

Smart dog. Dewey realized the specter hound must have smelled Beatrice's essence on the cursed spindle right away. "You did it," he said to the Hs. "You turned Beatrice Willoughby into a scarecrow."

"It was easy to lure her away from the rest of the party," Ms. H said. "Beatrice was a student of mine. She trusted me easily."

Dewey breathed sharply. The picture that Beatrice Willoughby had drawn—the one of the woman with her face crossed out—hadn't been a picture of the duchess after all, but of Ms. H.

"But why?" he whispered.

"We seldom pass up the chance to steal a child's heart," said the schoolteacher softly. "One a year. That's how we've stayed alive for more than two centuries."

Dewey's jaw dropped. "Two *centuries*—?"

Mr. H's eyes glinted. "Didn't you know?" he said. "People who absorb the magic of children's hearts look neither young nor old. We look *ageless*."

So that was why Dewey couldn't guess how old the Hs were. As he looked at their faces through his goggles, he noticed how unnatural their skin seemed to be: pristine and smooth, free of wrinkles, yet dull and heavy around the eyes, as if they had seen many unpleasant things over their lifetimes.

"You ate Beatrice's h-heart?" Dewey said, feeling sick.

"Don't be ridiculous, the heart has no use to us if

it's eaten," said Mr. H dismissively. "Its power comes from its being *alive*, just like how your heart is alive and stirring inside your body right now. So we . . . preserve it, you might say."

Next to him, Ms. H took out a bright-red apple from her pocket. Dewey, who had spent a lot of time picking ripe fruits from trees, could tell this was no normal apple. It was too perfect, with an unusual red sheen that practically glowed—just like the cursed spindle.

The Hs both looked fondly at the apple, and Mr. H murmured, "A child's heart teems with enough magic to give us an extra boost of life each year."

Dewey gaped at the glowing apple. "Are you saying that's an *enchanted heart?*"

"That's right," said Ms. H. "This is the heart of that silly boy from Amsterdam. I carry it with me so it doesn't get mixed up with the other apples on my school desk."

"I *told* her to turn the heart into a more distinguishable object, like shoes," Mr. H remarked. He shook his head and gave Dewey an amused look, as if sharing an inside joke. Dewey did not find the situation the least bit funny.

Ms. H admitted, "We got greedy when we selected

Beatrice Willoughby. We normally pick children who aren't from around here: kids of visitors and tourists, easily forgotten in a town where oddities happen regularly. Sure, we nearly got caught a few times. Those two kids claiming I locked them in a house made of *gingerbread*... imagine. All I did was offer them a piece of cake. Anyway, I suppose after getting away with something so many times, you become bolder. No matter, we won't make the same mistake again."

Dewey drew in his breath. So *that* was why the Hs were targeting him, he realized. Hardly anyone in town knew who he was, and his dad was no influential mayor or prominent figure. If Dewey disappeared, it would be forgotten within a week.

His hands were trembling. But he refused to let them know he was scared. "The hosts are already onto you," he said loudly. "That's why they invited you here tonight. Soon you'll be arrested, and Mort will be free!"

At this, both the Hs laughed. "As if anyone would remember us by the end of the night," Mr. H scoffed, twirling the cursed spindle between his fingers casually. He handed the spindle to Ms. H and clasped his hands together. "Unfortunately, that includes you."

They closed the door behind them and twisted the lock, trapping Dewey in the room. Dewey stepped backward, bumping into the writing desk. The specter hound lunged at Mr. H's leg, but being made of air and shadow, it did not leave any mark. In fact, it chomped its jaws uselessly while Mr. H tried to kick the creature away.

"We're thinking of releasing that boy from Amsterdam," said Ms. H. "His aunt appears to have ties to the city's police, and the last thing we need is an actual investigation. No, we want to swap him for someone from a more... *humble* family... like a traveling father-and-son duo with no real home, yes?"

"If I go missing, everyone in this house will know you did it," Dewey said.

"False," answered Mr. H. "If anything, this will only heap suspicion back on the Amadeuses. Another kid disappearing in their mansion, what a tragedy.... Maybe they'll arrest the entire family this time...."

Dewey looked around the study. There was no place to run. "Help, HELP!" he yelled at the top of his lungs.

The two grown-ups merely gave him an irritated look. "You've never been in a mansion before, have you?"

sighed Ms. H. "It's an enormous place. Unfortunately, nobody can hear you from downstairs."

Dewey hurried to the nearest bookcase. He clamped the hidden spindle between his teeth and climbed up, using each shelf like a ladder step. His hands were slippery from sweat, and he almost lost his footing a few times. With a grunt, he pulled himself to the very top. His goggles began fogging up, and he yanked them off to wipe the lenses on his shirt.

The Hs stood beneath him, looking faintly amused.

"It'll be over soon," said Mr. H. "After we take your heart, it won't hurt one bit. Of course, I can't say the same *during* the process. . . ."

There was a noise nearby. With a jolt, Dewey saw that Ms. H was trying to climb the shelf while Mr. H talked. Dewey hadn't even noticed her—the two were fading into the surroundings right before his eyes. It was only a matter of time before he lost track of them, before they ambushed like wolves hidden in the trees.

Dewey put on his goggles again. The Hs came into focus once more, both of them peering at him hungrily. The goggles must have deflected the Hs' natural abilities in the same way they had protected against Duchess von Pelt's hypnosis. Dewey made a silent promise that if he made it through this, he'd never take off his goggles again, no matter how many people teased him.

He leaned against the wall. With a grunt, he pushed the edge of the bookshelf with his feet. The shelf began to teeter dangerously. Ms. H let out a shriek. Dewey pushed again with all his strength. A moment later, there was a shattering crash as glass and hundreds of broken puppet pieces flew everywhere.

Dewey fell through the air. He managed to land on his feet—sort of. He tumbled across the ground, scraping his elbows and knees on the debris and twisting his ankle. Ignoring the tears of pain that flooded his eyes, he limped his way to the door. He saw, with a pang, the remains of the specter hound, fading away in a puff of dust under the debris.

"No—!" Dewey cried.

The creature let out one last silent bark before disappearing altogether.

Dewey wiped his eyes. Then he saw a pair of legs squashed beneath the toppled bookshelf; Mr. H was fervently pushing against the shelf, trying to reach Ms. H's crumpled body.

While they were distracted, Dewey unlocked the door and fled the room. He hobbled down the corridor. "Help!" he panted, keeping his voice just low enough so as not to attract attention from the Hs.

He reached the staircase. He was just contemplating how he was supposed to go down the narrow steps with a twisted ankle, when a tinkling voice said from behind him, "Try this way, it's faster."

Dewey yelled and whirled around, his heart pounding, but it was not the Hs who had spoken. A middle-aged woman with large eyes and pale skin smiled at him from a human-sized hole in the wall. For a heart-stopping second, Dewey thought she was a human puppet.

But then she tucked a blonde piece of hair behind her ear and spoke.

"I've been watching you, Dewey O'Connor. Pleased to make your acquaintance. I'm Maribelle Amadeus."

For a moment, Dewey simply gaped at Maribelle.

"That was a horrifying crash," Maribelle said, still smiling. "It'll take some time to clean up the study. No matter. Your pursuers are likely going to come around any minute. The passageways inside the walls are much faster. It's up to you." She spoke casually, as if they were discussing the weather or what they'd had for dinner.

Dewey glanced down the hall, then back at Maribelle. He wasn't sure he could trust her. "Why didn't you show yourself earlier?" he asked skeptically.

"The puppet master never reveals herself until the finale."

Dewey winced as he accidentally shifted his weight on his bad ankle. Maribelle gave him a sympathetic look and said, "I daresay dear Dr. Foozle will give you a cure for the pain."

"If I pay him," Dewey said with a grimace.

"I do encourage you to make a quick decision to join me."

After a moment's hesitation, he joined Maribelle inside the wall. Before he could change his mind, the wooden panels slid back into place, and the enclosed space was plunged into darkness.

"Not to worry," Maribelle reassured, heading down a hidden passageway. "Just follow the sound of my voice."

"I can see you with my goggles," Dewey said.

They walked through the tunnel, which was long and narrow. The walls pressed in against Dewey from all sides. He tried not to think about the spiders and rodents living in the crevices that Wormwood had mentioned earlier. The passageway twisted this way and that, sloping downward, then upward. Dewey clenched his teeth, pain throbbing through his ankle with every step.

Maribelle explained that she had been in these hidden tunnels many times, and that she could walk them with her eyes closed if she wanted. "Thanks to our nimble caretaker, I know all the secret nooks and crannies throughout the mansion. I was able to secretly observe everything that was happening the entire night."

"So this party was all your idea?" asked Dewey.

"Well, Mort and I planned it together," said Maribelle. "Loyal Wormwood dutifully helped us sneak letters back and forth from prison. It took years of research and plotting."

"And you knew the culprit... *culprits*... long before the invitations were sent out?"

"Yes. Wormwood has been spying on the townspeople for the last twelve years. He kept a careful eye on those who attended our party the night of the terrible Incident. Eventually Wormwood noticed that whenever children went missing, one of the Hs had been in the area immediately before or after."

"If you knew, then why didn't you tell the police?" exclaimed Dewey.

Maribelle brushed a spiderweb off the sleeve of her dress and shook her head. "That's just it. We didn't *know*. We suspected. The Hs were always very careful. That, and they're very *forgettable*. They fade into the background easily. But bats have a special ability that detects hidden objects through sound waves."

"Echolocation," Dewey said.

"That's right. The Hs could not successfully hide from him. Still, we knew it would take absolute, airtight proof to clear Mort's name," continued Maribelle, ducking to avoid a low-hanging ceiling. "But we had nothing on the Hs, and we were running out of time. We needed a judge with multiple witnesses to see firsthand how the Hs commit their atrocities. That's how we came up with the idea for tonight. We carefully curated a small guest list. I contacted your father to research each of the invitees far in advance. He's the only guest who was in on the plan."

Dewey exhaled. So *that* was why his dad kept ignoring his warnings—Chaucer already knew about the night's events. It would've been nice if his dad had filled him in. A lot of things would have made sense earlier.

As if reading Dewey's mind, Maribelle said kindly, "Your father was likely trying to protect you by keeping you in the dark. Adults often shield crucial information from children, thinking they might get afraid. But children are a lot stronger than we give them credit for. Case in point: yourself."

Dewey's face warmed from the compliment. "So, did you plant the scarecrow?" he asked. "And the dead crow in the cellar?"

"We left the scarecrow where we had found it," said Maribelle. "It really did give Edie's old room an unusual chill, and we didn't find it until she moved out. We found the crow a few years later—a stealthy one, that bird! He got tangled in some puppet strings and accidentally strangled himself, poor fellow, so we popped him straight into the icebox to preserve his body."

"But you could've shown those to the police!"

"Taking those items by themselves to the police station would have proven nothing," answered Maribelle. "We needed to tell a story for the evidence to make sense. A stage act, if you will."

"Each of the guests played a role tonight. . . ." Dewey said slowly.

"Yes. It was a gamble on how some of the guests would act. But Wormwood had studied everyone so closely, and we really felt this particular group, with its various quirks and abilities and hobbies and areas of expertise, was our best shot. All in all, I must say everything went according to plan *swimmingly.*" Maribelle gave a tinkling laugh. "The only hiccup was Wormwood revealing himself too early."

Dewey understood. *Maribelle, the puppet master.* They had been directed toward the final conclusion, like puppets pulled by strings. His heart thumped. For the first time, it all made sense.

That reminded him. "I'm sorry about your puppet collection," Dewey said sheepishly.

"Don't be. I can always make new ones." Maribelle's voice turned serious. "The real issue is, we only have fifteen more minutes until midnight. After that, I'm afraid the Hs run free, and Mort might stay in prison forever."

"We won't let it happen," promised Dewey.

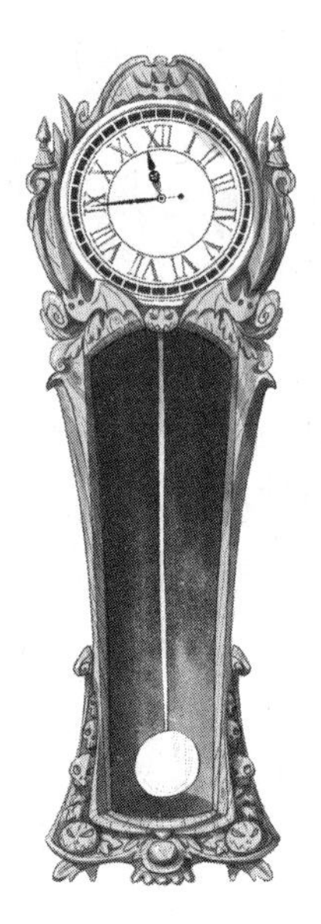

Chapter Twenty-One

FIFTEEN MINUTES UNTIL MIDNIGHT

Back in the dining hall, the remaining guests had reached a sort of stalemate: nobody moved, and nobody knew the next move.

"Oh crows, I guess we failed," said Mrs. Raven, staring at the grandfather clock. She supposed she shouldn't fret; she had found her long-lost friend, who cawed happily at her shoulder.

Chaucer sat up. "We can't give up yet!" he cried. "The Amadeuses placed a lot of faith in us."

"Ah, what's the point?" said Dr. Foozle, suppressing a yawn. "It's getting late." He wished he'd brought along a bottle of awakening draft from the pharmacy—coffee and tea simply were no match for the special brew he'd whipped up himself.

Judge Ophelius gripped his walking cane. "Four hours is not nearly enough time to solve a case," he said. *At least the infamous flower thief has been arrested,* he thought. A small consolation.

"An impossible task from the beginning," tutted Count Baines. It might've been possible if he hadn't been assigned such simpletons to work with.

"Come now," urged Chaucer, refusing to give up. The traveling story collector alone knew the truth. Yet for some reason, his mind went strangely blank when he tried to recall the real culprit (culprits?). "If one of us is responsible for Beatrice Willoughby's death, that person needs to face . . . what's the word? *Justice!*"

Judge Ophelius looked up at Wormwood, who was hanging upside down from the ceiling. "Please tell Mort and Maribelle we tried our best—" the judge started to say.

"*Hey!*" a voice called into the room.

Startled, Wormwood fell from the ceiling. He flapped back into the air.

"Chaucer, is that your son?" said Dr. Foozle, adjusting his spectacles and looking left to right.

For the first time that night, Chaucer noticed Dewey wasn't in the room. "Probably off reading somewhere, not to worry," he said. "He's a very independent boy." But a nervous flutter rose in his stomach. He hadn't been too worried about bringing Dewey along, not with the plan safely in place, but could he have been too... what was the word? *Careless?*

"Hey, up here! Dad!"

The guests looked up at the ceiling and gasped when they spotted Dewey's face peering through a vent.

"Dewey, come down here at once!" ordered Chaucer.

"Dad, I know who—AHHHH!"

The vent broke, and Dewey fell through the air for the second time that evening. Luckily, Maribelle had lightning-quick reflexes from years of puppetry. She grabbed Dewey's ankle (the nonsprained one), and he swung above the dining hall like a chandelier.

"Maribelle Amadeus?" gasped Mrs. Raven.

"Hello, hello, this wasn't quite how I wanted to make my grand entrance. . . ." Maribelle gave the guests below a strained smile as she struggled to keep Dewey from slipping further. "Wormwood, be a dear and help me, won't you?"

Wormwood fluttered over and grasped the boy's arm with his claws. "You're heavy," the bat grunted, but together with Maribelle, he righted Dewey and safely plopped him on the ground.

Dr. Foozle stepped forward, adjusting his spectacles. "Your ankle looks swollen," he remarked.

"I'm fine, but we don't have much time," Dewey said. He shifted his foot and leaned against one of the chairs. "Ouch!"

"What happened?" asked Chaucer.

Up in the ceiling, Maribelle clapped her hands, looking at the guests below. She flashed them a smile. "Right, then. I will let Detective Dewey explain everything."

Detective Dewey? Dewey blushed at the honorific. He

took out his notes that he'd jotted down that evening. The guests were quiet as he cleared his throat nervously several times.

"Ladies and gentlemen," he said, "as you all know, we've been invited tonight for a reason. In Mort and Maribelle's initial welcome letter, they mentioned one of us was responsible for Beatrice Willoughby's disappearance thirteen years ago. Any of us could have been the suspect. But we were also the detectives. And as the night went on, each of us helped the case in some way.

"First, Dr. Foozle, the expert on chemistry and magic, prompted by the clue of Beatrice's hair, conjured his specter hound out of bone dust—a rare substance he was told to bring ahead of time. With it we were able to track down the scarecrow and detect Beatrice's essence. From there, Count Baines used his ability to predict a hidden note, and we found the carefully placed riddle." Dewey turned to Wormwood and added, "I assume that was the work of you or Maribelle."

"Affirmative," Wormwood replied, flapping his wings. "I have a soft spot for poetry."

Dewey flipped through his notes and continued.

"The riddle then led us to the dead crow in the cellar. Mrs. Raven used her necrowmancer abilities to revive and translate the dead crow . . . the same crow she had brought to the party thirteen years ago. The crow had actually *seen* the people who had lured away Beatrice Willoughby and should've remembered their faces, but it couldn't. That was another clue."

The room was quiet. Judge Ophelius clutched his walking cane. Mrs. Raven clutched her chest. Count Baines clutched his pocket watch. None of the guests spoke; they stared at Dewey, speechless, as he continued to recount what had happened.

"Then, in the library, a particular book marked at a specific story led us to the theory that there was someone going around stealing children's hearts. This led to the conclusion that Beatrice Willoughby got turned into a scarecrow for her heart. Such work requires a cursed spinning wheel . . . and the only spinning wheel in the entire house is in Edie's room. So we knew one thing: someone had access to the spinning wheel and turned Beatrice Willoughby into a scarecrow that night. The Hs, being the only people Edie could not remember from the last party, went to ask Edie about her spinning wheel. Later, they presented us with the spindle from Edie's spinning wheel, which was glowing red and evidently cursed."

Oh, that's right. Most of the guests had forgotten who had shown them the spindle in the first place. Dewey only remembered because he had written down the names in his book.

"Speaking of which, where is the spindle now?" spoke up Dr. Foozle.

"I'll get to that in a moment," said Dewey. "As the night went on, I realized that all of us were taking other people's words at face value. A good detective confirms everything firsthand. So, with the help of the specter hound, I went back to Edie's room to reexamine where the evidence had come from. I used one of Edie's hairs to track down her essence. After doing so, I found the *real* spindle from Edie's spinning wheel." He fumbled in his pocket and held up the checkered wooden spike. "It was hidden back in Mort's study. Someone placed it there after we visited the room."

"So then . . . the Hs' spindle . . ." Mrs. Raven looked as if she'd swallowed a worm. "Oh *crows*."

Dewey nodded. "The Hs meant to lure us off their

trail with the cursed spindle, which they owned. But then, at that moment, Count Baines made a timely prediction that Duchess von Pelt would get arrested. We all got sidetracked after we thought she was the real culprit. But it turns out she wasn't—she was ultimately arrested for something else, unrelated to the case at hand."

Above them, Maribelle smiled and said, "I called in a tip to the police station about the tulip thefts and the duchess's whereabouts for tonight."

"Why?" the guests asked.

Dewey explained, "The hosts needed the duchess here because every good mystery needs a red herring, a person to throw others off the trail for a time. It's a good way to ease the minds of the real culprits, who would then believe themselves clear of suspicion."

"A very useful distraction," agreed Wormwood. "But it was risky. The police barely found the mansion in time."

Judge Ophelius glanced at Chaucer. "The random stories you told earlier—the story of the alchemist, the Magpie Spy, the disappearing family—they weren't random at all, were they?"

Chaucer, who had remained quiet, gave a small smile and admitted, "No, they were clues about each of the guests. I was hired by Mort and Maribelle to collect stories about each of you, to help keep the conversation going and your investigation's wheels turning."

Connected to one another by fine threads... Each of the guests were strands in the web, and at the center of it all was Beatrice Willoughby. The baffled guests blinked at one another as one more piece of the night made sense.

Judge Ophelius rapped his walking cane and demanded, "Where are the Hs now?"

"That's what I've been leading up to." In one breath, Dewey quickly explained how the Hs had chased after him, and how he'd sprained his ankle in the process.

Chaucer turned to Dr. Foozle. "Do you have a remedy for my son's foot?"

The pharmacist reached into his lab coat and took out a glass vial with dark green liquid. He supposed the kid deserved a treatment free of charge for clearing his name. "This should soothe your injury temporarily," he said, uncorking the vial and dabbing some of the contents on Dewey's skin.

A cool, icy tingle went up Dewey's leg, and he felt the pain subside. "Thanks," said Dewey gratefully.

"What happened to the Hs?" pressed Mrs. Raven.

"One of them's trapped under the fallen bookshelf in Mort's study."

"Wait," spoke up Wormwood with a frown. "Are you saying you *broke* Maribelle's puppet collection—?"

The broken collection was the last thing on everyone else's mind. There was a flurry of activity. The remaining guests quickly headed down the hallway. Dewey and Wormwood hurried after them.

They rushed up the narrow staircase and down the long corridor ("Can this house be any bigger?" grumbled Count Baines). Finally, they reached the study. Maribelle was already waiting beside the door.

The inside of the study was the way Dewey had left it, puppet remains and glass shards everywhere.

"Where are the Hs?" asked Dr. Foozle, adjusting his spectacles and peering at the mess.

Dewey stepped over a broken puppet with a gaping hole in its head and looked around. Through his goggles, he immediately saw Ms. H lying half buried under the bookshelf. Her body was limp, her ghostly white hand clutching the blood-red spindle.

Mrs. Raven leaned closer to examine the schoolteacher. Dead bodies and dead birds had startling similarities, the necrowmancer noted. After a moment, she stated mournfully, "She's not breathing."

There was a tense silence.

"Where's Mr. H?" spoke up Dewey.

"He's not here," said Maribelle. "He must have left before we got here."

"We would've seen him in the hallway," pointed out Judge Ophelius.

Dewey shook his head in dismay. "Not if we weren't already looking. That's what I tried to warn you guys about. The Hs have an ability to fade into the background."

"They were the only ones I had trouble tracking down stories for," said Chaucer, rubbing his beard. "But there are tales of the gruesome things they've done. Can't imagine anyone else was responsible for Timmy Weber, the poor little sleepwalker."

Wormwood tilted his head and raised his ear. Aside from his ability to navigate in the dark, the bat also had excellent hearing. He could hear the sound of mice moving behind the walls, the soft creak of the floorboards, or a pin dropping several feet away. "I hear someone one floor below us and ten doors down the hall," he said.

The group raced back downstairs. Dewey made sure his goggles were secure. The guests frantically searched the corridors. They looked beneath the staircase. They peeked under the furniture. They peered behind the paintings. Already, most of them had lost memories of what Mr. H even looked like.

"Can't you make another specter hound?" Judge Ophelius called to Dr. Foozle.

The alchemist shook his head wearily. "I'm out of bone dust. It'll be at least a month before I can make another batch to conjure that little guy again."

Just then, the clock chimed midnight.

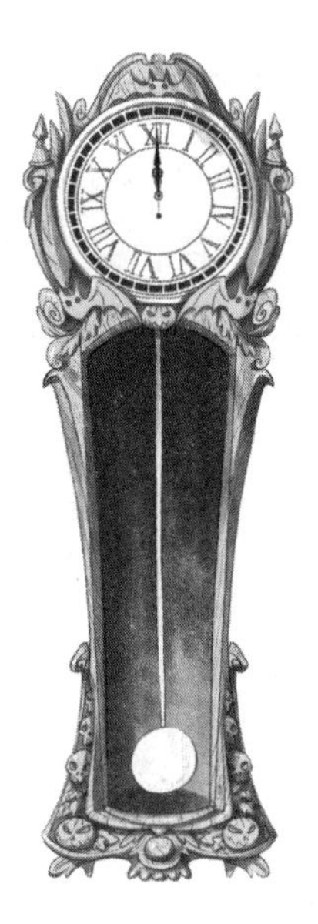

Chapter Twenty-Two

MIDNIGHT

A series of *click-click-clicks* echoed through the mansion. The group froze in the corridor on the first floor.

Wormwood explained, "The enchantment on the locks have lifted." Suddenly, the bat raised his head. He had heard someone moving near the front of the mansion.

By the time the group arrived at the foyer, all they

saw was the open front door and the pitch-black trees outside.

"Oh crows, he went free," said Mrs. Raven, shaking her head. The crow on her shoulder cawed sadly.

"Ah, I assume this is not part of the plan, letting him get away?" Dr. Foozle asked Maribelle.

Maribelle shook her head, a pained smile on her face. Dewey felt queasy, like the time he had eaten too many candied apples.

Judge Ophelius rapped his walking cane. The room fell quiet.

"It is unfortunate that one culprit has been squashed, and the other has disappeared," the judge said solemnly. "However, based on what I've seen and heard here tonight, I am convinced of Mort's innocence. I can't do much about Mr. H now that he's escaped...but I *can* do something about the wrongly accused. By the power vested in me, I officially exonerate Mort from all accusations and clear his name. He will be released from prison immediately."

Maribelle's eyes lit up. "Thank you, Your Honor," she said gratefully. Chaucer clapped, and the other guests gave nods of approval.

Dewey wasn't satisfied. "What about Mr. Whatshisname—Mr. H?" he insisted.

"I doubt the cobbler will stay in town after this evening's incident," Count Baines said.

Judge Ophelius nodded. "I will be alerting the authorities as soon as I can," the judge reassured everyone. "Although the statute of limitations for Beatrice's crime has expired, it is safe to assume that Mr. and Ms. H were responsible for the other disappearances around town. Mr. H, wherever he is, will not walk freely."

Maribelle glanced at Dewey, and the two exchanged a look of shared understanding. They both knew it was futile—Mr. H, with his special ability, would not get caught that easily. It had taken nearly thirteen years to plan the night's events. Dewey's shoulders slumped.

Chaucer reached out and pulled Dewey into a comforting hug. "Well done tonight, son," Chaucer said gently. "I knew bringing you along would help, with your vast knowledge. I think you make a fine detective."

"But one of the culprits got away," argued Dewey.

"True, but all is not lost. We cleared up multiple mysteries tonight, thanks to you."

"Thank goodness one of you humans has a brain," added Wormwood.

Mrs. Raven sighed. The crow on her shoulder seemed to as well. "Poor Beatrice Willoughby," the necrowmancer said. "If only I could bring her back to life, too."

Dewey, who had been slouched in defeat, suddenly raised his head. An idea began pulsing through his mind. "Actually . . . there might be a way." He flipped through the notes he had taken that evening, explaining his theory as he skimmed the pages. "The Hs told me they don't devour the hearts they steal. They store them, like trophies. And Ms. H said something about releasing the latest missing boy, the one from Amsterdam." He took a deep breath, his own heart beating excitedly. "What if that means . . . if we put Beatrice's heart back, we can bring her *back to life*?"

The others stared at him. "That is . . . oddly brilliant," gasped Dr. Foozle. "Like putting a battery inside an empty remote control."

Maribelle suggested they search the Hs' properties for the preserved heart. The judge stated he would need to issue a warrant first, which would have to wait until morning. But Wormwood merely winked at this and flew off. Within half an hour, the bat returned to the mansion, lugging a bulging sack of goods.

"Human laws don't apply to animals, Your Honor," the bat said shrewdly. "I stopped by the schoolhouse and the cobbler's store. I did not find any human hearts, but I tried to look for something that resembled a trophy." He spilled the contents on the floor for all to see.

A few guests raised their eyebrows. Among the items Wormwood collected included a brand-new box of chalk, a ruler, a patch of leather, and an old hammer. But one thing caught their eye: a pair of bronzed gown shoes with large diamonds on the tips, the kind that a princess (or a girl in a princess costume) might wear.

"Ms. H showed me an apple earlier," said Dewey, carefully picking up the shoes and examining their abnormally scarlet sheen. "They had the same glow."

"There were more all over his shop," said Wormwood. "Sneakers, ballet slippers, even a pair of ice skates. This was the pair that seemed likeliest to be Beatrice's."

"Those must be other children's hearts enchanted as pairs of shoes," remarked Count Baines. "How fitting for the cobbler."

Dr. Foozle rolled up his sleeves. "If this pair of shoes is indeed an enchanted heart, then it's possible to return it to its original state," he said. "It'll be difficult.... But then again, it is All Hallows' Eve, *and* I come from a long line of clever alchemists."

"I have no doubts about your abilities, Doctor," said Maribelle. "How much will you charge?"

Dr. Foozle adjusted his spectacles and didn't speak for several moments as he calculated the costs in his head. "I'll do this for free," he said at last, "in honor of all the missing kids the Hs have enchanted."

The group left him to tinker with his potions and magic. Mrs. Raven drank her eighteenth cup of tea. Chaucer, Wormwood, and Judge Ophelius sat by the fireplace, discussing the different laws in other places, and how the small town could borrow some of them to improve its own justice system. ("Otherwise, Mayor Willoughby's going to drown from despotism soon, Your Honor," said the bat.) It was way past Dewey's regular bedtime, and he was almost yawning as much as Count Baines, but he willed himself to stay awake to see if his idea worked, the same way he willed himself to stay up in order to finish the last chapter of a really good book.

It was early in the morning when Dr. Foozle ordered everyone to gather around. Glass flasks of all colors lay at his feet. The pair of shoes was suspended in midair, twirling slowly. Dr. Foozle's forehead was shiny, and he desperately looked like he needed a long night's sleep. But he grinned triumphantly and said, "Could someone bring down the scarecrow of Beatrice? Or I guess I should say, Beatrice herself."

Maribelle brought down the scarecrow from Edie's old room and gently placed it before Dr. Foozle. The guests watched as Dr. Foozle sprinkled some stuff on the bronzed shoes, then carefully pushed aside the straw in the scarecrow until there was a small cavity in the chest. He placed the shoes inside the hole... except now they resembled more of a lumpy, misshapen blob. In fact, it was no longer a pair of shoes at all, but a thumping human heart, veins throbbing right before the guests' eyes.

Before the others could take a closer look at the heart, the scarecrow began to glow brighter and brighter until all the guests had to shield their eyes and look away. When they blinked back again, what stood before them was no longer a lifeless scarecrow.

Judge Ophelius tapped his cane. "Perhaps we will make a call to Mayor Willoughby after all," he stated.

Word spread fast in the small town. The next evening, a summons was issued to every resident's mailbox by Mayor Willoughby, requiring that each person gather at the town square.

The townspeople were perplexed by the odd decorations that had been set up. "Those scarecrows are strange," said a boy to his mother.

A half circle of scarecrows stood in the middle of the square. The town mayor stood next to a scarecrow wearing a boy's cap and suspenders. He gave an emotional speech about his daughter, who had recently been found after being missing for thirteen years. Judge Ophelius stood next to the mayor, looking solemn. To the judge's other side was a man in a black cloak, looking slightly less solemn.

Mayor Willoughby neared the end of his speech. "...and I—I apologize to the Amadeus family," he grunted, giving a quick glance at the man in the black cloak.

The man merely nodded, but he winked at someone in the audience.

Maribelle Amadeus smiled back at Mort. Next to her, Edie sat silently in her wheelchair. Edie's mouth didn't move, but her fingers twitched, and words appeared under her embroidery needle. *About time that rotten man apologized.*

Maribelle suppressed a giggle and turned to the person standing on her other side, a boy in copper goggles, who was quietly explaining something to a young girl.

"Dr. Foozle is extracting the hearts from the bronzed shoes as we speak," he said. "Once the hearts are given back to their rightful owners, the scarecrows will come back to life. Count Baines is helping him match the hearts to the right scarecrows. His ability is handy for that kind of thing."

The girl's eyes were wide and curious. "They are all enchanted, like I was?" she whispered, staring at the scarecrows standing in the square.

"Yes," said Dewey. "Those are just the ones we've found so far around town. There are a lot more out there." He tightened the band around his goggles and proudly explained that he and his dad were planning to find as many enchanted scarecrows as they could on their travels in the next few months.

"And what happens to the two villains once the hearts are restored?"

"Well, one of them was squashed by a bookcase," said Dewey. "Dr. Foozle examined her body this morning, and he said she looked noticeably older. I'm guessing the same happened to the other one who got away. Remember, the enchanted hearts are what keep them alive. If we can find all the kids who got turned into scarecrows, and restore the children's hearts to their proper owners, Dr. Foozle thinks the two criminals should eventually turn into dust."

Beatrice nodded slowly, mulling over this information. "How many people does your caravan fit?" she asked.

"It can fit quite a few," said Dewey. "Why?"

"Can my dad and I come along?"

Dewey was surprised by the request. But he decided he did not mind Beatrice. Her boundless curiosity reminded Dewey a lot of himself—plus, she had not made fun of his goggles once. "Sure, if it's okay with my dad and yours," he said.

Chaucer had no problem with this, either. It took a bit of convincing to get Beatrice's father to agree.

"Absolutely not," was Mayor Willoughby's initial response, and he puffed his chest angrily in that familiar manner of his.

"Please, Daddy," insisted Beatrice. "I want to help free the children who were trapped by the Hs like I was."

"It's too dangerous," the mayor said firmly. "I'm not risking my life traveling the world to who-knows-where."

"It'll be no less dangerous staying in this town," said Judge Ophelius. "One of the culprits escaped. He's still out there."

Beatrice motioned to Dewey and the others who had been at the Amadeuses' residence. "If it weren't for them, I would still be a scarecrow," she said.

"I would still be locked away unfairly," piped up Mort nearby.

Mayor Willoughby grimaced. The events of the last twenty-four hours had pressed the usual pomp and greed out of him. He knew he owed the Amadeuses and everyone who had helped restore his daughter. Still, he wasn't sure he wanted to spend the rest of his life squeezed inside the O'Connors' tiny caravan. It was already a shock finding Beatrice alive and well after all these years. The mayor had grown accustomed to a life without kids, and it hadn't taken long for him to be reminded of how exhausting children could be with their endless energy and incessant questions.

At long last, to everyone's surprise, Mayor Willoughby agreed to let Beatrice go on her quest with Dewey and Chaucer, as long as she called home once a week and visited often.

"We will take good care of her," promised Chaucer. "She'll be quite useful in our search, since she has been a scarecrow herself!"

"We'll bring justice to all the missing kids out there," added Dewey earnestly.

As the others discussed packing lists and preparations, Maribelle pulled Dewey aside.

"I just wanted to thank you for everything again," she said. "My family . . . the entire town . . . we owe you more than you can ever know."

Dewey shrugged, embarrassed. "It's not a big deal. Really." He added, "I'm disappointed Mr. H escaped."

The thought of the cobbler, whose face Dewey could hardly remember, tingled in his mind like an itch that he couldn't scratch. They had been *so close* to catching him.

Maribelle smiled. "You know, Dewey," she said, "all

the greatest detectives have a nemesis. Sherlock Holmes and Moriarty, for instance."

With that, she reached into her pocket and took out a tiny marionette, smaller than all the others in her house. This one was newly made; the paint still smelled fresh. The tiny figure held a pair of boots in one hand.

Dewey took the puppet and studied its face. Slowly, his spirits lifted. He returned Maribelle's smile. He would meet Mr. H again—he was sure of it.

One Year Later

Mrs. Raven waved at the father-and-son duo that stepped off their caravan. "Good evening!" she called, a fresh pie under her arm. "How was your trip here?"

"It was long but good!" Chaucer replied cheerfully. "We might stay in town for a week or so. Any chance you have extra rooms at the Nevermore Inn?"

"Oh crows, we're fully booked... but I will see to it

a room is made available. The Nevermore Inn is your home. You and Dewey are welcome to stay however long you wish. Where is Beatrice?"

"We dropped her off at her father's house for the evening. He will be proud—she helped us find three scarecrows last month! It was . . . what's the word? *Fortuitous.*"

"It wasn't just pure luck, Dad," corrected Dewey. "We had an ample set of clues leading us on the right trail."

They headed into the Inkwoods together, following the new, glittering stone pathway that led to the mansion. The woods were full of chatter that night; large groups of people were walking alongside them. A few feet away, Duchess von Pelt, dressed in a great big dress stitched with pink peonies, was chatting with Count Baines.

". . . and I was so glad that Mort and Maribelle finally took up my advice for the party decor," the duchess was saying. "Especially now that they're opening up the parties to everyone again, it's *crucial* they make a good impression. . . ."

Count Baines merely nodded, looking bored and glancing at his pocket watch now and then. "Avoid drinking the punch in ten minutes," he said to one of the guests walking near them. The guest gave him a startled look.

At the front door of the mansion, an elderly woman in a wheelchair greeted the guests. There was a crinkle of a smile on her wrinkled face. A gray bat was perched on her armrest. She nodded at the robed man who passed them.

"Great of you to make it, Your Honor. Or—sorry, should I say, *Mayor* Ophelius?"

Several other guests did a double take. They could've sworn it wasn't the old woman who had spoken, but the bat perched on her wheelchair.

Mayor Ophelius bowed his head. He no longer wore his white curled wig. "Thank you, Wormwood," he murmured. "The new title still takes getting used to."

"I hear the local authorities helped a tourist find her missing umbrella the other day," Wormwood said approvingly.

Mayor Ophelius smiled. "I am glad they've become more helpful. If there are any other suggestions for improvement, please let me know."

"Oh, I undoubtedly will. Human governments are fascinating."

Down in the dining hall, the hosts were busy serving their guests tea. Dr. Foozle took a cup from Maribelle, thanked her, then went back to his conversation, in which he was explaining his latest concoction to several interested listeners.

"Add just a few drops, and your shoes look clean as new. Ah, it only leaves a small side effect: your big toe might turn slightly turquoise, but it's temporary. Interested? I do take credit cards." One of the guests asked him a question, and Dr. Foozle laughed nervously. "Yes, of *course* it was approved by the health board—er, it's in the process of being approved, anyway. . . ."

"Speaking of shoes, have you met the new cobbler?" asked one of the guests. "Started up his shop recently. He's quite experienced."

"About time," said another guest. "The town was in need of a new one."

"I'll say," agreed the town postmaster. "Mail keeps piling up addressed to a Mr. Hamelin, but there's no one in town by that name."

"Ah, how curious," said Dr. Foozle. He had a vague memory of what had happened to the previous cobbler—something about him running off with the previous schoolteacher and disappearing from town, maybe? It had all happened so long ago. "That's good. I need the soles of my shoes mended."

Down the hallway, one of the guests walked quietly through the chatting crowds. He walked slowly, because his legs were no longer as sprightly and young as they had once been. Nobody detected his presence, and if they accidentally bumped into him, they'd smile apologetically and say, "Sorry about that, Mr.—uh, Mr.—"

"Forget about it." The cobbler smiled.